The Disappeared

BY

CATHY MACPHAIL

A TYLER LAWLESS MYSTERY

It was the cool breeze that woke me, blowing against my face. I opened my eyes slowly. It was too dark to make out the place where I was lying. All I could see through a broken window were clouds drifting across the starlit sky. The floor was covered in dust. There was rubble all around me. I could feel the grit rub against my cheek. From somewhere in the shadows behind me I heard voices. Men's voices, I couldn't make out what they were saying. They sounded harsh, angry, threatening. I was in danger; that much I knew. What was I doing here? How did I get here ? And where exactly was 'here'?

Those men meant me harm, no doubt in my mind about that. I edged away from those voices as silently as I could... and then I gasped with fear. I was balanced on the ragged edge of a huge hole in the floor. It swirled down to blackness. One more inch and I would be over. Desperate to get away from that hole I moved back, too quickly, made too much noise.

I felt a foot placed firmly on my back. Holding me down, pressing me down, hurting me.

' Like the view, Tyler? Hope so, because that's where you're going....'

I could see no face. Only hear a man's voice that sounded almost friendly but there was menace in it. He pushed me closer to that hole with his foot. I tried to grab at anything I could, but there was nothing to hold on to , only rubble and dust. I struggled. How I stuggled. But it was hopeless. I toppled over. I felt myself going down, and down. The ground was rushing up to meet me.

I was going to die. I was going to be one of the unlawful dead I was meant to help.

I began to scream.

And I woke up.

My mum ran into the room. ' What on earth, Tyler!' she threw herself on the bed, put her arms around me. ' Were you having a bad dream?'

I was cloaked in sweat, breathing hard. ' It was terrible, mum, terrible.'

She hugged me. ' I've never known anyone to have dreams like yours. '

I wanted her to hold me forever. I had been so afraid. A dream, I told myself over and over, it was only a dream.

But the thought wouldn't go away.

It wasn't a dream.

It was a premonition.

CHAPTER 1

I'd almost forgotten about Miss Baxter, the dead teacher from my old school, the one I had seen all those months ago. So much had happened since then. I'd moved to a new school, St. Anthony's, met new friends, changed people's deaths. Changed the past. Yes, changed the past. I had that gift, if it was a gift.

Ben Kincaid, Sister Kelly, my Gran, all these people, their destiny had been changed because of this gift I had. But I'd put Miss Baxter, the teacher who had died in Crete, the one who had started it all, I had put her almost to the back of my mind, until that day, the day after that terrible nightmare, when I was on my way to school and I saw her again.

I was on the early morning bus. It was packed with other pupils, or with workers heading for their offices and their shops. My head was stuck in a book as it usually is. I wasn't aware of anyone around me until I looked up as the bus jerked to a stop. The bus was no longer packed. In fact, it was almost empty now. There was a little girl, maybe nine or ten, two rows in front of me, kneeling round in her seat, smiling at me. Freckles dotted her nose. Her black hair was held back in a clasp. I smiled back, and she giggled. Her mother tugged at her arm to turn her round, and she did, but a moment later she had swivelled round to me again. This time she didn't smile. She just stared at me with her bright blue eyes. I smiled again, but she just kept on staring.

I don't know about you, but I hate it when children do that. They seem to have the knack of being able to stare, never taking their eyes from you, and never blinking. They can do it for ages, and after a while, you just have to look away. Pretend you don't see them. Look anywhere to get away from that unblinking stare.

That's what I did after a while. I felt as if my grin was fixed to my face and she was beginning to give me the creeps. I turned my eyes to the street outside. The bus was coming to a halt again. At the bus stop, there was a long queue of people waiting to come on.

And there she was in the middle of them. Looking as solid, as much flesh and blood as anyone else on the street. Miss Baxter, the teacher from my old school, Grovepark, who had died in a tragic accident. The first ghost I had ever seen.

Here she was again. As if she had been waiting for me. Waiting at that bus stop just for me. I felt the colour draining from my face. She was staring right at me. She looked just like all the other people who were waiting there. Not like a ghost at all. She was wearing a white blouse, the kind she used to wear to school, the collar turned up.

Her dark red hair was pulled back from her face. Too tightly, it made her look harsh and cold. No doubt in my mind. It was Miss Baxter.

But Miss Baxter was dead.

No one else was aware of her. They filed past her as if she wasn't there. And she wasn't. Not for them.

She was only there for me.

I slid closer to the window, pressed my face against the cool glass. Miss Baxter lifted her hand. She held it out to me. And though I couldn't hear her voice, I heard her words as clearly as if she was standing right beside me.

' Help me, Tyler.'

It was what they all asked. ' Help me, Tyler.'

I smacked my hands against the glass. I wanted to get off the bus, but it had already started to move.   Her eyes never left me. Her silent whisper still followed me. ' Help me, Tyler.'

And then she was gone.

' Help me Tyler.' I knew what she wanted me to do. What they always wanted me to do. Stop them from dying, save them, change their past. Miss Baxter was one of the unlawful dead, and it was they, it seemed, that I was able to help. The people who shouldn't have died, because it wasn't their time.

I don't know how, or why I had been given this gift, but Miss Baxter knew I could do it. Miss Baxter, the first to ask me, had waited long enough. I knew I had no choice. It was time to help her.

Trouble was, I didn't have a clue how to start.

CHAPTER 2

Jazz was waiting for me at the school gates, studying her nails, chewing gum. She had been kind of abandoned by Aisha, now that she and Callum had got together. It had brought Jazz and I closer. She looked up as I stepped from the bus.

' You're white as a sheet, Tyler.'

I so wished I could tell her about Miss Baxter, but who would ever believe such an unbelievable thing?

Then she added. ' You look as if you've seen a ghost.' I tried to laugh about it but I couldn't have been very convincing.

' Have you?' Jazz loved the mysterious. And though she knew nothing of my gift, I had a feeling she understood there was something different about me. And it came to me then, that perhaps I could tell Jazz. After all, once I changed the past, brought Miss Baxter back from the dead, Jazz would remember nothing about it, and it would be so good to confide in someone.

' I thought I did,' I said.

She grabbed at my jacket and began jumping all over the place. ' Tell me, tell me, tell me!' She pulled so hard one of the buttons on my jacket flew off and bounced on the path.

' Sorry,' she said, picking it up and handing it to me. ' But this is so exciting. You saw a ghost!'

I pulled her towards the lake outside the school. It was almost autumn, yellow leaves still clinging to the trees, late flowers in bloom. We were well hidden here.

' You remember I told you about that teacher in my last school?'

She nodded. ' The one that got you expelled. The dead one you kept seeing?'

' I wasn't exactly expelled...' I wanted to remind her. I simply left before I was pushed. But there was no use explaining it now. ' Yes,' I said. ' That one.'

' You...saw her... again...this morning...on the way to school?' A big breath almost between each word. No question, no disbelief. Jazz even stopped chewing.

I had told people before, and become a laughing stock, a joke. I couldn't go through all that again, the whispering, the giggles behind my back. If I told Jazz even a bit of the truth, she would be the only one. 'I think I saw her again this morning,'

' You're psychic, Tyler. I've told you that before.' Jazz linked her arm in mine. ' If you're seeing her , there has to be a reason. How did she die again? '

' Her car went over a cliff. It was a tragic accident.' I repeated the phrase everyone had used at the time. It was how the papers had described it. *'A tragic accident.'*

Jazz tutted. 'Ha! Bet it wasn't. I watch these programmes about ghosts coming back all the time, Tyler.' And she did. She revelled in them. ' And they come back for a reason. She might want you to find out exactly what did happen to her. '

' Her car went over a cliff in Crete. What's to find out?'

She dismissed that. ' But she's back for something, isn't she?'

The bell rang. We began to hurry to the school. ' You won't tell anybody, Jazz. Promise?'

She smiled, showing her bright white teeth. ' Not even Mac?'

Mac was kind of my boyfriend. The very first boyfriend I had ever had. We only ever went out together in a crowd, but I was happy with that. He was the last one I wanted to know. So afraid he might laugh, turn away from me. Think I was weird. The way everyone in my last school had.

' Especially Mac. Jazz, it has to be a secret.'

She shivered with excitement. ' Ooo, I love secrets,' she said.

' Anyway, maybe I won't see her again.'

' You'll see her again,' Jazz said. Not for the first time I thought that Jazz was perhaps the really psychic one. ' If she wants something that bad, she'll be back."

CHAPTER 3

There were moments that morning when I remembered the reason I hadn't wanted to confide in Jazz. ' Don't tell anyone,' I had said. And, as always, she was true to her word. She said nothing to any of our other friends. However, she kept turning to me in each class, winking at me, or putting her fingers to her lips as if she was buttoning them, to let me know how much I could trust her.

Finally, as we left Geography, Aisha held me back. 'Okay, what's going on?" she asked. " What's all this?' And she put her fingers to her lips mocking Jazz.

Jazz had the cheek to look surprised. Not just surprised, but offended too. Her mouth went round like the moon. ' We don't know what you mean,' she said, looking at me. ' Do we, Tyler?'

' I'd like to know what's going on too,' Mac said, coming up behind us. He looked at me, with those deep brown eyes I always felt I could drown in. ' What's the big secret?'

The last thing I wanted was for Mac to think I was keeping secrets from him. Though my darkest, deepest secret I could never tell him. That one, he could never know. He had already found out what had happened in my old school, what a fool I had made of myself there. If it all started again, he would lose interest in me. I was so afraid of that.

I struggled to find a lie that he might believe. Not so the bold Jazz. Why is it some people are so good at coming up with lies?

' Goodness, you spoil everything, Mac.' She let out a deep sigh. She touched my arm. ' Looks like we're going to have to tell him, Tyler.' I was totally baffled. Then her accusing eyes went back to Mac. 'We were talking about having a surprise party for you actually-as it happens.'

Mac's birthday was in just a couple of weeks. I had almost forgotten about it. How did she come up with these things, and so quickly? You had to admire her.

Mac's face broke into a wide grin. ' Honest? ' he said. A surprise party for me? I love surprise parties.'

Jazz grabbed me by the arm, swooping up Aisha as she swept us along the corridor. ' It's not going to be much of a surprise now, is it?'

As soon as we were alone again, and were out of earshot of Aisha, she whispered. ' You do realise we're going to have to organise a real surprise birthday party for him now, don't you?'

CHAPTER 4

Jazz insisted on coming home with me that day. I live on the other side of the town, a good distance from Jazz and Aisha, and I could see Aisha watch us going off to the bus stop together. She looked puzzled and a bit hurt I thought. She was feeling left out, and I had been left out often enough to know the feeling. For a moment I wondered about telling her too, drawing her into my secret. But I knew Aisha disapproved of ghost stories, only believed what could be proved. So I said nothing, just waved at her. I still wasn't sure if I'd done the right thing telling Jazz.

She dragged me up to my bedroom as soon as we were in the door of my house. ' To talk strategy,' she said. She was loving every minute of this. She closed the bedroom door and immediately suggested a séance.

' I've been thinking about this all day,' she said. ' Let's try and get in touch with your Miss Baxter.'

' That's not how it works, Jazz,' I told her.

' How what works? ' She lifted a black eyebrow.

How could I tell her the truth? That the dead, the unlawful dead, came to me, asked me for help. And they didn't need a ouija board to do it.

I wished I could think as fast as Jazz sometime. ' I just think a séance would be a waste of time.'

Jazz had settled herself on the bed. I was sitting cross legged on the floor. Anyone coming into the room would think the bedroom belonged to Jazz, and I was the visitor.

'Why has she come back? ' Jazz said. ' That's the first question. She must need something. I think she needs you to find out how she died.'

' But she died in Crete, Jazz, I can't be expected to go to Crete to investigate.'

' Of course you don't have to go to Crete. Haven't you heard of the internet? You can find out anything you want there. In newspapers, on travel sites. But if you do have to go....I'll go with you. I've always wanted to go to Crete.'

' First time I've heard about it,' I said.

Jazz didn't even answer that. ' Maybe she went out there with a boyfriend, and they had a terrible fight and she went off driving like a crazy woman, and whoosh! Over the edge of the cliff.'

She made me laugh. ' I thought I was the one who made up stories!'

Yet, she did make me think. I knew nothing of that final holiday Miss Baxter had taken in Crete. Did she go alone? Or with friends? Or did she indeed go with a boyfriend?

Jazz read all that on my face. ' You're wondering that too, aren't you? Okay, first thing we have to do, is find out exactly how the accident happened.' She began counting on her long nailed fingers. Bending each one back with the index finger of her other hand. ' We have to find out who she went on holiday with, and why she chose Crete? Why not Spain, or Italy? There might be a clue in that too.' Her face beamed with delight. ' This is so exciting. I am so glad you told me. And I promise I won't do any of that stuff I did today. I won't do it again. I will be the soul of discretion....'

She went rattling on, but her voice seemed to fade into the distance. I hardly listened. All I could hear were Miss Baxter's words. ' Help me Tyler. '

I didn't know how I was supposed to help her. But I knew I was going to try.

Jazz was ready to go onto the internet right then to find out more, but my dad popped his head round the door and offered her a lift home.

' An offer I can't refuse,' she said, and she whispered as she said goodbye that she'd find out what she could tomorrow.

I slept that night, though I thought I wouldn't. I was sure Miss Baxter would come again, her image forming in a dark corner of my room. I knew now she wouldn't come to scare me. She would come to remind me not to forget her.

' I won't, Miss Baxter,' I whispered, ' I won't forget you.' And I slept peacefully all that night.

CHAPTER 5

Next day after school, I visited the library. The library was an old one, in the centre of town. A Carnegie library, full of atmosphere, with alcoves and dark corners, and nooks and crannies, and a huge domed glass ceiling. Every visit was like a step back in time. I loved going there, searching the bookshelves, taking in all those peculiar smells you associate with old books. Of course there were loads of computers there now too. Computers I could use to look at the old papers and the reports of Miss Baxter's death.

It was quiet when I went in. There were a few elderly people searching for books, some students on computers, children tugging at their mothers' skirts . I was looking for books about Crete. I wanted to see the island Miss Baxter had visited, the place where she had died. I took the books to a quiet spot out of sight of everyone. There was a table and chair in one of the little alcoves, I settled myself there and set about reading.

It seemed to me that Crete was a perfect island for a holiday with its white beaches, spectacular scenery, and its history. It was even the home of the mythical minotaur, although the guide book assured me there was no longer any there. Why shouldn't Miss Baxter have chosen here for a holiday? And when I saw photographs of the deep gorges and the mountain roads and the plunging drops to the sea, I could see how easily a car could go over the edge. No wonder there had been that ' tragic accident.' A corner taken too fast, on a dark night, a driver unused to driving on the right hand side of the road would have no chance of regaining any control.

I was so caught up in the book I didn't notice the little girl by my side. I looked up. The girl smiled. She was about ten, with black hair held back in a clasp. It took me a moment to realise she looked familiar.

She recognised me too. ' I saw you on the bus, didn't I?' she said. " Yesterday. Do you remember?'

The little girl with the unnerving stare. Then I smiled too. ' Yes, I remember you.'

'Do you live near here?' she asked.

' Not really. But I like coming to this library, it's good isn't it?'

' We've just moved here,' she said, ignoring my question. ' We lived far away, and then we moved here. It's a long walk to this library.' She rattled on. ' None of my friends live anywhere near here. There's my mum...' She turned and looked down a long line of bookshelves, but there was no one there. ' Oh, she was there a minute ago.' She turned back and peered over my shoulder, studying the book I was reading.' Are you going on holiday?'

' No,' I shook my head. ' I'm just reading up on Crete.'

' Crete,' she said, and I wondered if she even knew where it was. ' I'd love to go there. We go to Scarborough every year. Have you ever been there?'

' No,' I said. ' Don't think I have.'

' You should go. It's brilliant...better than Crete.'

She chattered on, hardly waiting for any of my answers. She'd just moved here, I told myself, she was probably lonely.

' What's your name?' she asked me.

' Tyler,' I said.

She beamed a smile at me. ' Tyler, that's an unusual name. I like it. I've got such an ordinary name. Anne.' She scrunched up her face as if she was smelling something nasty. ' When I've got a little girl, I'm going to call her Tyler.'

She pulled a small oblong box from her schoolbag. ' Look what mum bought me today.'

It was a little lacquered box, about the size of a long envelope, engraved and painted in bright colours. She opened the lid and music began to play. I recognised the tune. Carousel. That had been the last school show before my humiliating departure from Grovepark. I had been in the chorus.

' I'm going to keep all my treasures in there,' Anne said. ' Look. My mum gave me this.' She held up a dangling silver earring.' She lost the other one. And look at this.' She picked out a silver coin , held it up for me to admire. ' It's an American dollar. Mum always kept it in her purse, but she gave it to me. Have you got anything you could give me Tyler?'

I thought perhaps it might be the only way to get rid of her. I patted my pockets. ' Don't really think I have anything....' then I found the button. The green button that Jazz had pulled from my jacket. I could give her this, I thought. Mum had already sewn on the spare button. I didn't need this one. ' It's not much of a treasure though.'

If she was disappointed, she hid it well. She almost snatched it from me. ' Yes, it is. I love it. Green's my very favourite colour.' And she put it into the box, and carefully closed the lid. The music stopped. 'Thank you,' she said.

Just then a woman appeared, peering round the bookshelf looking a little annoyed.

' Is that your mum?' I whispered .

She looked up. Waved. ' Hi mum,'

Her mum completely ignored me. ' There you are, Anne. I told you to stay close by. Come on, we're going home.'

Anne smiled back at me as she moved off. 'Bye Tyler, I hope I see you again,'

' Me too,' I said. Not quite meaning it. I had a feeling that I might never get rid of Anne if I was too friendly.

I watched her skipping back to her mother. The woman pulled at her hand roughly, and she looked back to where I sat and seemed to scowl at me. 'Who were you speaking to, Anne?'

' Tyler, mum. Her name's Tyler.' I heard Anne say.

I could just picture Anne getting into trouble for speaking to strangers, even if the stranger wasn't much older than Anne herself. But then, the news all this week was about a child going missing, snatched from his pram in a park. Out of his dad's sight for only a moment, and he was gone. So it wasn't hard to understand that she didn't want her daughter talking to strangers.

I watched them leave the library, and I went back to my reading.

The ringing of my phone seemed to resound around the walls, and up into the domed glass ceiling. I took it out of my pocket. I saw it was Jazz's number. The librarian stepped between the bookcases and gave me a shattering look. She pointed to the sign.

ALL MOBILE PHONES MUST BE SWITCHED OFF.

I felt my face go red and I jumped to my feet as I answered it, and headed for the door and the foyer.

Jazz was chattering away, excited about something, but I couldn't listen. Not until I was safely in the foyer, with the door behind me closed and then I had to ask her to go over again what she had been saying.

She let out a cry of exasperation. ' Didn't you hear a word I said, Tyler. It's about your Miss Baxter. I just found out. It was all kept very hush hush, but the rumour was that it was no accident. Your Miss Baxter committed suicide.'

CHAPTER 6

' Are you still there?' Jazz asked.

I was still trying to take in what she had just told me. Suicide?

' I think I know now why you saw her,' Jazz bubbled on. ' She's stuck here. It's hard for her to get into heaven because she killed herself. Bet she feels guilty.'

' So why is she bothering me?'

That only stumped Jazz for a second. ' Maybe if she killed herself in Crete, so far away, her parents don't know why she did it. Maybe she wants you to tell them. I remember seeing that in an episode of Medium.'

' This isn't a tv programme, Jazz' I said. She didn't understand. How could she ? ' How come nobody knew this? There wasn't even a rumour about suicide at my old school.' And I should know, I had listened to them all. And then another thought struck me. ' And how come you found out, Jazz?'

I could picture Jazz shrugging her shoulders, tossing her head back. ' My mum knows half the people in this town, and the other half know her.' Her voice grew soft. ' As soon as I mentioned your Miss Baxter,' she went on quickly when she heard I was about to interrupt her. ' Don't worry, I didn't tell her why I was interested. Anyway, I'd hardly got the words out of my mouth when my mum says...' Oh, you mean the lassie that topped herself on holiday?"

I could see where Jazz got her way with words.

' My mum says it was all kept really quiet, but my mum's second cousin was their home auxiliary for a while and she says Mrs. Baxter was devastated. Ended up in the mental hospital. Psychiatric problems, well, that's what they called it, if you know what I mean. But it seems your Miss Baxter was really depressed when she went on that holiday.'

I still couldn't understand. ' She surely didn't go on holiday just to kill herself.'

Jazz sighed. ' Maybe she went on holiday to try to cheer herself up, but it didn't work, she was on her own, and that only made things worse, and that's why she killed herself?'

No, I thought, she went to Crete for a reason. Something happened on that holiday that made her take her own life. . But it all had to do with what was happening here before she left. Those phone calls I had seen her make so often, standing in corners, whispering, her hand over the phone, her face grim.

' Miss Baxter's back , Tyler,' Jazz said. ' And she's back for a purpose.'

25

CHAPTER 7

I wandered back into the library. I was even more confused than ever. How was I supposed to help Miss Baxter? How could I stop her from dying, if it was what she had wanted to do herself? Was Jazz right? Was I meant to find out why she'd committed suicide? Help her parents to understand the reason she decided to kill herself? How could I possibly find out what had happened in Crete? She would have to come back to tell me. Nothing else for it.

As if in answer, the library grew dark. Clouds scuttled across the domed glass of the roof. It was as if the volume had been switched off. The library was silent. I knew what was happening. She was answering me.

My eyes scanned the library looking for her.

And there she was, sitting at one of the computers. She looked up at me. I'd always thought her pretty, but now I saw she was almost beautiful. Her eyes were huge and blue, her face framed with a cascade of long red hair. In school, she'd always worn it in a tight roll, making her look so severe.

' Help me, Tyler.' Her voice whispered to me across the library.' Help me.'

' But how?' I pleaded. ' You wanted to die. You killed yourself. How can I change that?'

She looked to the computer placed her hands on the keys. ' Help me,' she said again, and then in the blink of an eye, she was gone.

Things moved back to normal. Sounds came back to the library. A baby crying, an old deaf man shouting at the librarian for a book he could not find. But no Miss Baxter.

But I had a feeling I knew what she wanted me to do. Find out about her accident on the computer. I sat where she had sat in only moments before. The screen was opened at the front page of today's local newspaper. It was all about the missing child, a local headline as well as a national one. Maybe, I thought, she wanted me to find the coverage of her death in this paper. Maybe there was some kind of clue there.

I flicked through all the past editions till I found the paper from the week she died. Even then, it was hard to find any article about her. Only a tiny edge of a column.

LOCAL TEACHER DIES IN CRETE

Popular local teacher, Barbara Baxter, was killed in an accident while on holiday in Crete. She lost control of her hired car as she was driving down one of the steep mountain roads. Miss Baxter had been alone at the time. Police say there are no suspicious circumstances.

No suspicious circumstances. No hint of suicide, or of anything more sinister. There was nothing here. Nothing I didn't know already. What was it she wanted!

And all at once, I felt her presence again. Almost as if she was hovering behind me, reading the article too. The library grew cold. I wasn't the only one to feel it.

' Somebody's opened a door.' A man shouted to the librarian.

It was as if a gale force wind rushed into the library. Books toppled from shelves, papers flew from the librarian's desk. Magazines were flung from stands and scattered around the floor.

' What's happening?' a woman snatched her baby up in her arms. ' What on earth is happening?"

And then the computers flashed on, one by one, their screens filled with static, the swivel chairs in front of them began to spin, round and round.

I heard Miss Baxter, though I couldn't see her any more. I heard her voice so clearly. And her voice was angry now. ' Help me! You have to help me!'

And I shouted back, forgetting myself. 'I don't know how to help you! I'm trying!'

The mother with the baby moved away from me. ' Who are you talking to? '

People were all looking at me.

A man at one of the computers, got to his feet, began backing away from me. ' What's she doin'!' he yelled . ' What are you doin'!'

'It's not my fault!' I shouted at them. 'It isn't me!'

But no one believed me. I could tell by the alarm on their faces, the fear. It was as if the library had come alive, books tumbling from shelves, computer screens glowing, a wind that came from nowhere, and it was me who had caused it. But it wasn't me, it was Miss Baxter. She was furious with me. I had done something wrong, and she was angry.

I put my hands over my ears and ran.

CHAPTER 8

Miss Baxter had been responsible for what happened in the library.   I remembered her sudden bursts of temper when we had done something wrong in class. It was as if that had happened in the library. But what was it that I had done wrong? I ran all the way home. Wishing I could leave all of this behind me. Why me? All I wanted was to be just an ordinary girl. The only worry I would have was getting my homework in on time, or gossiping about who was going to win the X factor.

This was a curse I had been given, not a gift. Or maybe I just wasn't clever enough to know how to handle it. I slammed my way into the house. All was quiet. Mum and Dad had gone out for a meal, and Steven, my brother, was working late.

I stood in the hall, listening to the silence. Waiting for Miss Baxter to form before me, fury in her face, expecting that she had followed me. She would never let me go. They never did let me go. But after a few moments I realised that she wasn't here. She wasn't coming. The house was empty. I flopped on to the stairs, trying to think what to do next. What did Miss Baxter want me to do?

I remembered how often I had seen Miss Baxter making those furtive, at least to me they were furtive, phone calls. Closing over the phone when she saw I was watching her. I had thought at the time she was calling a married boyfriend, that she was embarrassed at me catching her. Now, it seemed it might have been something else. She certainly hadn't gone on holiday with any boyfriend-unless she had met him there. She had been alone in the car.

To begin with, Miss Baxter had been one of the most popular teachers in the school, always with a smile on her face. Almost overnight, all that had changed. Her smile had vanished. She'd become short tempered, morose. I wasn't the only one who had noticed that.

And then, she had gone to Crete. Alone. And she had killed herself.

I would have to find out why.

My phone ringing made me jump. I thought it would be Jazz, but it was Mac. I felt myself melt when I heard his voice. I'd never even liked boys before I met him. I still couldn't believe he liked me too.

' What was wrong with you today, Tyler?' It made me smile listening to him. How Scottish he sounded. No one would ever think that voice belonged to a second generation Pakistani. ' You were walking about in a dream.'

' Was I?'

' Thought you'd fell out with me,' he said.

' No! I would never do that.' I said it too quickly. Nothing cool about me.

' Dreaming about me, were you?' I laughed, though that would usually be true. Dreaming about his deep brown eyes. I wished I had a smart answer for him. Jazz would have had one. But I couldn't. I felt my cheeks go red even though he couldn't see me.

' Are you working out the details for this surprise party of mine?'

His party. Oh dear, I had that to think about too.

' Well, just so you know, Callum's up for being the dj.'

' Callum?' I had never even known Callum to be interested in music.

' Yeah, you know Callum. Mr. I Can Do Anything.' He laughed, we all knew what Callum was like.

' Well, that's the music sorted then.'

After Mac had rung off I felt so much better. Ordinary, real life can do that to you. I opened up my computer and clicked into the internet.

Miss Baxter had died only a year ago. Yet, I found it hard to find any details about her death. No interviews with her parents. No photos. But there was so much other news at the time. There was a banking crisis, a foiled terrorist plot, and these stories had taken up all the major news. When I did find her story, it was in one of the middle pages and once again only warranted a column.

A tragic accident.   No mention of suicide. No mention of suspicious circumstances. A young teacher had died in a tragic accident while on holiday. End of story.

But I knew it wasn't the end of the story.   There was something Miss Baxter wanted me to find out. And she would give me no peace till I had discovered what that something was.

CHAPTER 9

I called Annabelle that night. I hadn't spoken to her in ages. Once we'd been inseparable-best friends- whispering all our secrets to each other. Now, she had found new friends, and so had I.

She didn't even recognise my voice at first. ' Tyler?' A pause, a deep breath. ' Oh, it's you.'

Another pause. Not knowing what to say. ' How's things?' I asked her.

I could imagine her in her bedroom, with its bright pink wallpaper, the posters of Take That pinned on every wall. But perhaps it was all changed now. Not pink anymore, another pop group had perhaps overtaken Take That. She said suddenly, as if she was trying to break the silence. ' Liz and me are going off on the school trip in a couple of weeks.'

' Liz? Liz Cole?'

I could almost hear Annabelle blush. Sorry she'd brought her into the conversation. Liz Cole- I still hurt with the memories of how she taunted me because I had told everyone I had seen the ghost of Miss Baxter. Getting me into trouble because I had whispered to her, of all people, that I thought the French mademoiselle and the science teacher were having an affair. She'd gone straight to the head, I'd been branded as a troublemaker, always eavesdropping. ' Sleekit' they had called me. I'd never liked Liz Cole, and neither had Annabelle. Now, it seemed she was her best friend?

Embarrassed, Annabelle stumbled over her answer. ' Yes, Liz Cole...you remember her? Honestly, she's really nice, Tyler. Not the way we used to think at all.'

I could never believe that, but I said nothing.

Annabelle rattled on. ' She's changed since that accident she had, remember on that school ski ing trip to Aviemore?'

I remembered. She'd had a bad fall, smashed her leg badly.

' It ruined her chances of being a gymnast,' Annabelle went on, trying to explain. ' That was her dream. I felt really bad for her, Tyler. It turned her into a totally different person.'

As if it was an excuse for her choosing Liz as her friend.

' I would have thought that would have made her change for the worse,' I said.

' Oh no,' Annabelle said quickly. ' She was broken hearted, Tyler, and I felt so sorry for her, everybody did, and after you left, her and I...well we just.....' she stuttered to a halt. ' She is a really nice person, Tyler.'

Really nice person? Liz Cole would have to have a personality transplant for that to be true. Anyway, I wasn't interested in Annabelle's new best friend. I needed information.

' Annabelle, you remember Miss Baxter? Do you know anything about how she died?'

Impossible not to hear her long sigh. ' You're not still on about that, are you?'

I had known that would be her reaction. My story had already been prepared. I wasn't about to tell her I had seen the dead teacher again. ' I'm writing an essay for our next test, a teacher who inspired you.'

' When did Miss Baxter ever inspire you? You were hardly in any of her classes.' The sneer in her voice had a definite Liz Cole touch in it.

It was true, though, what she said. Miss Baxter was never any kind of special teacher to me, but I decided to ignore it. ' I thought it would be a nice tribute to her. She...she died in that car accident in Crete, didn't she?'

There was a hesitation. ' This isn't going to be anything about a ghost, is it, Tyler, because that will only get you into trouble all over again.'

' It's nothing to do with a ghost.' I know I snapped at her, but Annabelle was beginning to annoy me. I was wishing I hadn't phoned her at all. ' It's a tribute to her, I told you. It's going to be a really nice essay.'

Her voice softened. ' Sorry Tyler. I just think maybe you should pick another teacher to write about.'

My tone changed too. We'd been such good friends. I could surely trust her. ' That's really why I called you, Annabelle. I wanted to check something with you, before I started it....' I cleared my throat. ' I don't want you to tell anybody I'm asking this, promise you won't tell anyone.'

She sighed again. ' I promise...what is it?'

I drew in my breath. 'I heard a rumour that it wasn't an accident at all, that she might have....killed herself...have you heard that?'

' Tyler!' The warmth left her voice. ' I've never heard anything like that. Who told you that? You can't write that in an article! What are you thinking about?'

' Calm down, Annabelle. I'd heard that and decided if it was true I would never write the essay. I was just asking!'

But she wouldn't calm down. ' Will you never learn, Tyler. Why don't you just let Miss Baxter rest in peace! '

' I was only asking a question. I thought since you were supposed to be my best friend once upon a time, I could ask you, in confidence! but it seems I was wrong. Okay! I'm sorry I phoned you!'

' So am I!' she snapped out,. ' You're a nutjob, Tyler.'

' I've been called worse.' I reminded her, but she'd already switched off her phone.

That night I dreamed of Miss Baxter. Such a pretty teacher, with her dark red hair and her bright smile. Her smile had disappeared near the end. Then she had gone to Crete, and she had died. Had she committed suicide? Was that because of something she had found out there?

In my dream she was coming closer to me, heading towards me-reaching out for me-begging me to help her.

And I was backing away, I was terrified. Shaking my head. Saying NO! and I couldn't understand why I was so afraid, so reluctant to help her. She was pleading with me, and I was saying- ' NO! NO!' As if I knew something terrible would happen if I helped her.

I woke up, awash with sweat. My dream was warning me not to help her. It would be the wrong thing to do...and I couldn't understand... why?

CHAPTER 10

By morning these fears that had kept me awake half the night, seemed groundless . I had promised myself that if someone came to me for help, one of the unlawful dead, as my Aunt Belle called them- then I would help. I wouldn't refuse. And in the bright light of a sunny morning I knew that was what I had to do. It had only been a dream, after all.

Maybe I wasn't meant to stop her dying, not this time. I hadn't stopped my beloved gran from dying, but I had given her the extra days to live and bring a serial killer to justice. Maybe Jazz was right. I was meant to find out why Miss Baxter had killed herself and pass that on to her family.

That morning, a Saturday, before I met my friends in the Mall, I walked to Miss Baxter's house. She had lived with her parents, in a little semi detached house in the West End of the town. Her house was not far from Grovepark. There was a gang of girls who adored her. We called them The Baxter Bunch. They used to make a point of walking past her house, giggling, hanging round her corner. Pestering her. Copying her. I used to wonder why she didn't move

The street was quiet, except for a couple of people working in their gardens, and a window washer perched on a ladder. Mr. Baxter was there in his garden. I recognised him from the funeral. Most of Miss Baxter's year group had attended. The sobbing Baxter Bunch overacting, while the rest of us sat quietly, not quite knowing what to do. His hair was greyer than I remembered, and he was thinner. He was bent down to a rose bush, clippers in his hand. He must have been a keen gardener, because I knew he worked in the local garden centre .

I stopped at the gate of the house, and it was a moment before he looked up and noticed me standing there. He stared at me. Didn't smile.

' Can I help you?'

 Why had I come here? I felt my face go red. ' I was one of your daughter's pupils,' I said quickly.

He began to nod. ' Ah, you're one of those girls who used to come here, are you?' He thought I was one of the Baxter Bunch. ' Nice of you to remember her.'

His friendly tone gave me courage. ' I'm writing a piece about her for an essay I have to write...teachers who have inspired me.' I said it as if it was really true. Where did I learn to lie like that?

His face broke into a smile. ' Oh, that is so nice. Thank you.'

I should have felt guilty but I didn't. I was trying to help his daughter after all. ' I wondered if you could tell me anything about her, something personal, that I could put in?'

He stood straight, put a hand against his back and stretched as if he ached. ' She was always a good daughter, always wanted to be a teacher.' He looked into the distance, a hint of a smile on his face, as if there was a memory there. ' Even when she was a wee girl she was always playing at schools.'

' She was a really good teacher,' I said, and that wasn't a lie.

He nodded. ' Yes, she was.'

' It was so sad that she died so young.'

' A tragedy. It was a tragedy.' He let out a long sigh.

' Why did she go to Crete? I've always wondered.'

The wrong thing to say. He looked at me. The smile was wiped from his face. ' What do you mean...why did she go to Crete? It was a holiday. Just a holiday. What else would it be?'

I began shaking my head. ' I just meant... I thought....I wondered why.. Crete? '

' It was a holiday. That's all it was.'

There was a hint of panic in the way he said it.

' I'm sorry, I thought...'

' What kind of essay are you really writing...what's your name?'

I didn't want to tell him that, though I was sure my name had never been mentioned to him when I got into all that trouble at Grovepark.. The headmaster had kept all my stories well away from him and his wife. The Baxters were going through enough, he told me. If they heard about me at all, I was simply 'that troublemaking girl.'

' Maybe I could talk to your wife?' I said.

He moved toward me so fast I stumbled back. ' Don't you go near my wife. I don't know what your idea is, but don't you come back here at all. And don't bother writing anything about my daughter. I forbid it!'

He stood watching me as I hurried away, making sure I was leaving. But my journey hadn't been wasted. I had learned something. There was a reason Miss Baxter HAD gone to Crete. Mr Baxter's reaction told me that. It told me more than that too. He didn't want me to find out what that reason was.

I turned the corner and almost fell over the little girl, Anne, once again. She was sitting on a wall, swinging her legs. She was wearing little white socks and black patent shoes, always so prettily dressed, always so neat. She jumped from the wall when she saw me. ' Tyler!" her face beamed in a smile.

Anne always seemed to turn up when I was thinking of Miss Baxter. Why?

I looked around for her mother. She followed my gaze. ' Mummy's gone to the shop. She'll be back in a minute.' She gestured to the little corner shop.

' I don't think your mum would like you talking to me, Anne.'

She didn't even disagree with me. ' I know,' she said. ' I don't know why. You're so nice.'

' It's because I'm a stranger, Anne. Your mum doesn't know me. You have to be careful.'

' Never take sweets from strangers!' she said at once. ' I know. A little girl got snatched, did you know that? Taking sweets from a stranger. I'd never be that stupid.'

It had been a little boy, but I didn't bother correcting her. I sat on the wall beside her. ' Did you live far away?'

She nodded. ' Dumfries.' She said. ' It's awful, awful, awful far away. I was sick on the bus coming here.' She added that bit proudly.

' And left all your friends behind? I know that feeling.'

' I know, I really miss my friends.'

' You'll soon make more.'

She giggled. ' Make friends. I think that's funny. As if I can knit them, or build them with bricks.'

I laughed too.

' Anne!' the voice was harsh. Anne jumped from the wall. She stopped smiling.

I looked up. It was her mum. She obviously had just come out of the shop, a drab woman, I thought, who looked older than she probably was. ' Come here now!'

Anne looked from me to her mum. ' But mum, I want to talk to Tyler.'

' I said, come here now!'

I would have offered to speak to her mother, but she looked as if she would shout at me too. 'Go on Anne, do what your mum says.'

She skipped back to her mother who snatched at her hand angrily, then looked back at me with annoyance in her face. Why, I wondered, was she always so angry at Anne ? Did she never smile at her, praise her? But then, a child had gone missing, younger than Anne, but still a worry for any parent. Perhaps that was why she always seemed so tense.

I was meeting Anne for a reason. I was sure of it. I was meant to help Anne too. I just didn't know yet how.

CHAPTER 11

Two days passed and nothing happened. No sign of Miss Baxter, and Jazz was so disappointed. She was never done asking me.

And then, the call came. I was sitting in my bedroom doing homework. I heard the phone ringing in the hall below. It was our Steven who answered it. Then he called out for dad, and when dad went on the phone, there was immediately something in his tone that made me sit up and listen.

Dad's voice was a murmur at first, then it grew harsher, and louder. Finally he shouted for me, and there was no softness in his voice at all. ' Tyler!'

He was standing by the fireplace when I walked into the living room. Hands by his side, fists clenched. Not like my dad at all. Almost comical, looking like some stern Victorian father. ' Okay, what's all this about?'

I was baffled. ' What's all what about?'

' That was the headmaster of your old school on the phone. Mr. Adair.'

I felt a chill running through me.

' He seems to think you're up to your old tricks.'

My old tricks. I knew what he was talking about now- that was what the headmaster had always called my interest in Miss Baxter. He must have found out about my visit to Mr. Baxter. I tried desperately to think of a good reason for my going there.

If only it had just been that. But it was much worse .

' What on earth are you thinking about Tyler. Spreading rumours that Miss Baxter committed suicide!'

That took me completely by surprise. ' I haven't. I didn't….I only….'

Dad lifted his fists. ' Tell me you never said a word about suicide to anyone, and I'll believe you. I want to believe you.'

He waited, and my hesitation told him everything. He slapped his brow. ' Tyler! What the hell are you doing!'

Dad ranted on and I never said a word. I was too busy thinking. I had only mentioned the fact I'd heard Miss Baxter had killed herself to one person. Annabelle. So little of a friend now that she was quick to pass it on. Spread it around like muck. I felt angry and betrayed.

' What made you say such a thing?'

How to explain it? ' I had heard there was a rumour…I only…'

Dad didn't give me a chance to finish, though I had no idea what to say anyway. ' Why are you bringing all this up again? Why now? It nearly broke your mother's heart the last time.'

And there was nothing I could say. No explanation was possible, nothing he could believe anyway.

' I'm sorry, dad.' I didn't want to hurt them, to hurt anyone.

'Sorry, isn't good enough.' Dad said. ' The Baxters have been really upset about it.'

That took me aback. ' You mean, he told them about it?'

' I don't believe he had to. Rumours have a habit of spreading, Tyler.'

My dad never spoke to me like that. It scared me.

' Can you imagine how hurtful that must be, to hear a rumour like that? They're just getting over their daughter dying, in a terrible accident, and now you suggest something so awful."

Now I snapped back at him. ' I wasn't the one who suggested it. It's a rumour I heard, okay!'

' So who told you this story?'

I hesitated. I wanted to shout out. ' It was Jazz, she told me.' But of course, I couldn't. I bit my lip, said nothing. Dad shook his head. As if he didn't believe I had heard it from anyone. The rumour had started with me.

' And no matter how awful you just had to pass it on.' He took a deep breath. ' I don't want to hear another word about this Miss Baxter. It's finished. Done with. Over ! Is that clear? I have promised Mr. Adair that is the end of it. '

I stomped upstairs. I was angry. Angry at Annabelle who couldn't keep her mouth shut. Angry at Jazz for telling me in the first place. Angry at my dad. But most of all angry at Miss Baxter. She had got me into so much trouble before, I had ended up almost being expelled. And now it was starting all over again.

I slammed the door of my bedroom. And I yelled and didn't care who heard me. There was only one person I wanted to listen. ' I don't care what you want me to do! Forget it. I 'm finished with you. I don't want any part of this anymore. Go find somebody else to help you!'

CHAPTER 12

I sat in my room, rocking myself back and forth, hugging my knees. What was that old phrase, I'd read it in some Robert Burns poem we'd been forced to learn. I hadn't understood it till now.

"Nursing her wrath to keep it warm."

That's what I was doing. Nursing my wrath, keeping it warm, building it to boiling point and getting hotter by the second. Going over again and again, the unfairness of it all.

Miss Baxter had appeared to me before and caused me no end of trouble. Here she was back. She came back because she knew I had the power to help her. But I didn't know how. I was new to this gift, and it seemed to happen in a different way every time. And anyway, if she'd chosen death for herself, *was* she one of the unlawful dead? What nerve to come back and ask me to change that when it had been her choice in the first place!

I was angry at Annabelle too. I had confided in her, trusted her. I would have trusted her with my life. Once. As my anger grew I knew I was going to call her.

By the time I punched her number into the phone I was ready for a fight. She answered at once. She clearly didn't recognise my number. She certainly didn't expect it to be me. I could tell by the way her voice trembled as soon as she realised who it was on the line.

' Oh...Tyler...how's things...?' You can hear guilt in someone's voice, can't you? It poured through the phone like slime. Annabelle knew why I was calling.

' My dad had a very nasty phone call from your headmaster, Annabelle.'

Annabelle! Stupid old fashioned name. Called after her old granny, she had once told me. I had thought it so sweet . Once.

Now I hated it.

She said nothing. Guilt written all over her silence.

' Did you hear me!' I yelled it.

' It wasn't me,' she mumbled. ' Honest ,Tyler.'

' It wasn't you? You were the only person I mentioned it to. I asked you not to say anything to anyone. You promised.' My voice was rising with every word. ' So you must have told someone, did you have the whole school laughing at me again. Having a good laugh, were they, at weird old Tyler.'

' I didn't tell anyone...' her voice was a sob as if she was ready to cry. The actress in her, always knew how to get round people. She used to do the same in class. Her eyes would fill up whenever a teacher would give her into trouble, and then they would all soften towards her. I knew all her tricks.

' So, how did it reach the headmaster. He reads minds does he? And the Baxters too.'

' The Baxters!'

' Yes, the Baxters. Did you really think it wouldn't get back to them?'

' Oh Tyler, I didn't know the Baxters had heard it.'

' And you still say you didn't tell anyone?'

She hesitated. And that told me everything.

' Who did you tell?" But I knew the answer before she spoke again.

' But Liz wouldn't...'

' Liz Cole. You told Liz Cole of all people. You know she hates me. All she ever did was try to get me in trouble, and you told her! And then she blabbed it all over the school. How was I ever a friend of yours Annabelle?'

When Annabelle spoke again, the softness was gone. So was the guilt. She was as angry as me. 'Because I was the only one who would put up with you, Tyler Lawless. The only one who stuck by you when everybody else was avoiding you because you were SO WEIRD.'

She screamed the last words.

And she wasn't finished. ' And you're still weird. Well, Liz Cole isn't. She doesn't do weird things. She doesn't say weird things.'

' No, not weird. Just wicked!'

' Maybe she shouldn't have passed it on. But you said it in the first place. So what is it this time, Tyler. Miss Baxter popped up in Tescos again, has she ? Tell her I was asking for her. You deserve everything you get.'

' Fine by me. And you can pass a message on to your new best friend. Tell Liz Cole, I'll get her for this. You see if I don't.'

CHAPTER 13

I promised myself that night that if I saw Miss Baxter again I would ignore her. Let her find someone else who would help her. I couldn't be the only one who could change the past, could I? Let her pop into any old séance and ask a medium to do her dirty work. But not me.

Why should it be me?

Jazz and Aisha were waiting for me at the gates of the school when I arrived next morning. They were all excited. ' Guess what!' Jazz said. ' We've found the perfect venue.'

' Venue? ' Aisha giggled. ' Have you swallowed a dictionary, Jazz? She means the perfect place.'

I looked blank. ' Place...for what?'

Jazz let out one of her dramatic sighs. ' For Mac's party, what else?'

Mac's party. I was doing nothing about that. They were doing everything.

' Mac's party. Remember?' Aisha said. Her face crumpled into a frown and I had the distinct feeling they had talked about my lack of interest in it.

I didn't blame either of them being annoyed at me. From now on I would concentrate on Mac's party. Nothing else. After all, I had finished with Miss Baxter, hadn't I? I smiled. ' So, where is it going to be?'

' Our church hall,' Jazz beamed. ' Wee Father Brady said it's free, the usual bingo night's been cancelled. And he's quite happy for us to use it.'

I laughed. ' A party for a Muslim boy in a Catholic church hall....now that's integration!'

' And we even have a DJ.'

' I know!' I said.

Callum popped up behind her. ' And luckily, I'm free too.'

We all began walking up the drive toward school. 'And since when have you become a DJ?" I asked.

' Lifelong dream,' Callum lied. ' Since last Friday! I've got a lot of CDs..."

Aisha laughed. ' He's got three.'

Adam came up behind us. ' You've got to have the patter too, Callum. Get everybody up dancing.'

He began dancing around us and singing. ' Let's get this party started! Let's get this party started!'

' If you're trying to look cool, it's not working. You look as if you're having a fit,' Jazz said.

' Leave it to me, I'll be fantastic.' Callum said, very confidently. 'Cometh the moment...cometh the man.'

' And Mac doesn't know a thing about it!' Mac jumped in front of me, and my heart beat a little faster. Couldn't help it. ' And don't forget the cake.'

' I'll bake it,' Jazz said,' and we all gagged.

' Death by chocolate takes on a whole new meaning,' Adam said.

' Thomas the Tank engine or Mickey Mouse? 'Aisha asked.

' Star Trek,' Mac said. ' Do they do a Star Trek cake?'

' They will,' I promised. ' If I have to make it myself!'

He flicked me under the chin. ' That's my girl.'

This was how I wanted my life to be. Laughing with my friends, organising parties, having a boyfriend like Mac. I would not let anything interfere with it.

In class, Jazz leaned across to me. ' Are you in trouble at that old school?" she asked .

' Do you know everything?' I whispered back.

' My Auntie Ellen knows one of the cleaners there. It went round that whole school like the flu. I don't know why you told that blinking Annabelle for anyway. You might have known she'd have to tell her new best friend.'

' I know, but I can't blame anybody else. I shouldn't have even mentioned it to her.'

' It was my fault.' Jazz said. ' I told you about that suicide thing. I mean...it wasn't a lie. I want you to know that. It's true. It's one of the main reasons the mum fell apart after she died. But I didn't mean for it to get you into trouble.'

' No, it wasn't your fault. It was mine. I should have kept my big mouth shut...'

She said very softly. ' Any more sightings of...you know who....?'

' I'm going to forget about it. It got me into too much trouble the last time, and it's doing the same again.'

She shook her head. ' You won't be able to forget it, Tyler. The dead teacher won't let you,' she said in a spooky voice.

I had a feeling she was right.

CHAPTER 14

Mac walked me to the bus stop after school. ' You seem a bit pre-occupied. Is anything wrong?'

Had he heard of the trouble I was in? I hoped not. But Jazz knew, why not Mac?

' Nothing's wrong,' I said, maybe a bit too quickly. I wasn't sure that he believed me. He knew of my reputation at my old school. He'd played football there and there were lots of people delighted to tell him about weird old Tyler. But I had done nothing weird in this school. The memory of all that had happened with Ben Kincaid had been wiped out when I had changed the past. I didn't want Mac to think I was weird now.

' You've not gone off me or anything, have you?'

' No, no.' I sounded desperate, and I blushed. ' No, don't think that, Mac. There's nothing wrong. Honest.'

The bus left me on the main road, and it was still a bit of a walk to my house. I strolled up the tree lined streets, past fine grey tenements. The afternoon was muggy.

Warm, with hardly a breeze, but with dark clouds thick in the sky. It would rain later I thought.

' Tyler!'

I turned round and there she was, once again. Little Anne. She came running towards me, dragging a school bag behind her.

' Is this where you live?' I asked her.

' Yes, over there.' She pointed a finger at one of the tenement blocks. I couldn't tell which one she meant. They all looked the same. ' Can you come and meet my mum?'

I remembered her mother's glare when she saw me last. I didn't think she would be happy to see me now.

' I have to get home, Anne.'

She looked disappointed. ' Aw, I've been hoping to meet you again.'

I had a moment of gratitude that Anne didn't live too close by me.

' How are you settling in?'I asked her.

She lifted her shoulders . ' I really miss my friends.'

' You'll soon make new ones. I remember when I moved schools, I left all my friends behind, I felt really lonely.'

' That's just how I feel, Tyler.'

I felt suddenly sorry for her, remembering my own loneliness. ' Well, do you know what? I've made lots of new friends, and they're better than the ones I left behind.' Annabelle sprung to mind. ' Give it time, Anne, the same thing will happen for you. Look on it as an adventure.'

She let out a big sigh. ' You always make me feel so much better. I wish I had a big sister like you.'

' Don't you have any sisters or brothers?'

She shook her head. Her clasp loosened seemed to hang from a single hair. She pulled it free. ' I did have a sister....she died...and now, there's only me.'

No wonder her mother was so protective of her. But I shouldn't feel sorry for Anne, I thought. She seemed to come from a caring family. Her mother might look harsh, but she obviously loved her. She was just lonely, this little Anne, but that would change.

She took the little lacquered box from her schoolbag, she must take it with her everywhere I thought, and she opened it . The music for Carousel chimed out again. She placed the clasp very carefully inside.

' More treasures?' I asked her.

She held the box out to me. ' I've got even more now. Look.' She picked out a small silver bangle. ' I had this when I was a tiny baby. My mum lets me keep it in here. She knows she can trust me to look after it,' she said proudly. ' I take care of things, she says.' She beamed me a big smile, proud of that achievement. The silver ring went back and out came a small handmade Christmas card. ' I made this at school. In primary one.' I had a look at it. Still in pristine condition.

' You really do know how to take care of things, Anne.'

She put it back carefully. ' Mum says years from now I will be able to show these to people, and tell them the story behind every one of the things in this box.'

' That's right, you will.'

She took out the button I had given her. ' This is my favourite.' She positively glowed with pleasure. 'It's beautiful. I'll keep it forever. I promise. Thank you so much for giving it to me.'

She came close and hugged me, and I felt so sorry for little Anne. Always so alone. So grateful for such a tiny thing as a plain green button.

She placed the button in the box as if it was as precious as gold. Then she closed it carefully.

I watched her skip back down the street, and step into one of the tenement closes. She turned and waved back to me before she disappeared.

Why did I keep seeing this little girl? There had to be a reason why I kept meeting her. Her sister had died? Was that it? Was I going to meet up with that sister at some time in the future, and save her from dying...so that perhaps Anne would never be lonely again?

My mind was so filled with these thoughts as I walked along that tree lined street that I almost didn't see her. Miss Baxter. Standing just ahead of me on the pavement. Waiting for me. Watching for me.

I stopped dead. I would ignore her. Turn away from her. Hadn't I promised myself that was what I would do?

Her voice came floating toward me, as if it was carried on the breeze. ' Tyler, you have to help me, please.'

I wanted so much to shout back. NO! To tell her I was finished with her.

But I didn't. Of course I didn't.

And when Miss Baxter beckoned me to follow her. I did.

CHAPTER 15

It was as if I was moving into some kind of dream world. Miss Baxter passed through an archway in the street, which led into a residents' car park behind new flats. I followed her. But when I stepped through into the light, my eyes were blinded by the sun.

I looked up. There was not a cloud in the sky. Yet, only moments before, the sky had been filled with them, heavy dark clouds. Now, the sun was out. There was no breeze, and it was hot.

I knew in that moment, that I was in another place, another time. I looked around for the teacher, and there she was, Miss Baxter walking through a bustling market in the square of a small village. She was not a ghost now. Now she was alive. She looked as I had never seen her, with her hair flowing down her back. She was wearing a wide brimmed sun hat. She was wearing shorts too, and her legs were nut brown from the sun. She had big colourful holiday bag slung over her shoulder, just like any normal tourist. She moved from one stall to another, fingering silk shawls, lifting pottery, studying handmade jewellery. I wandered behind her, and no one saw me.

I was the ghost- as I had been so often before. A ghost in the past. Invisible.

Why had she led me here, to this place, to this moment? There had to be a reason.

She stopped at one of the stalls, as if she was admiring the bright scarves displayed there. I moved closer so I could see her face more clearly. She looked distracted, and it was clear then that her eyes were not on the scarves at all. They kept darting round as if she was looking out for someone. For a moment she turned and looked right at me, and I stepped back behind one of the stalls as if she might see me. Still not used to this invisibility thing. Of course, she didn't see me. And after a moment she walked on.

I was ready to move to follow her when I heard a low growl. A skinny, half starved mongrel of a dog appeared from behind one of the stalls and was barring my way. I moved aside, and its eyes followed me. Its growl became a bark.

The dog could see me.

Now it began jumping around wildly, barking madly. It seemed afraid. Afraid of me. The bark turned into a whine. It cowered, its tail between its legs. Miss Baxter looked round when she heard the noise. Everyone did. But no one saw me. All their eyes were turned on the dog.

A woman came running from the stall. She grabbed the dog by the collar, and looked all around, as if she was wondering what could have scared him. Her eyes passed over me, unseeing. I tensed. She finally dragged the dog away. Its wild barking had stopped everything and it took a moment for people to turn back again and get on with what they had been doing. When I looked round, I thought I might have lost Miss Baxter in the crowd, but she was standing beside a little yellow European car. The front door was wide open. I thought she was leaving at first, but no. She put a parcel in to the passenger seat and a moment later she closed the car door, and moved back into the little square where the market was situated. Her eyes were still looking all around, as if she was watching for someone.

I was ready to follow her, wasn't that what I was there for? Follow her, find out who she was meeting, who she was watching for?

But my eyes were caught by a dark figure stepping out of the shadows behind one of the whitewashed houses. He looked every inch the tourist. His mop of dark brown hair flopped over his brow, and he was tanned, and was wearing an open necked blue shirt, khaki trousers. He was handsome, apart from a long white scar that ran the length of his face. There was something about him that made me stop and follow his gaze. He was watching Miss Baxter . She was climbing the steps of the little blue domed church, along with many other tourists. She put a mantilla on her head before she stepped inside, and was lost to my sight. I turned my eyes back to the man.

He stopped for a moment, his eyes still on the door of the church, as if he was waiting in case Miss Baxter might come back out. When she didn't, he began to walk to her car. It was parked in the shade, under trees, out of the glaring sun, in a quiet part of the car park. He looked around as if he was checking to see if anyone was watching him. No one was. Only me. The market was busy. A tourist bus had just driven in to the small square, and the passengers were flooding out. I was the only one aware of what he was doing. In one quick movement he bent flat under the car, and I knew in that second what he intended.

He was going to do something to Miss Baxter's car. Something that would cause her to lose control, and crash.

I had to stop him. I ran towards the car, I even banged on the hood. But there was no sound. My hands made no sound. I had to stop him, but how? What could I possibly do? In this world, in this time, I was invisible.

But not to everything.

I glanced across to the stall where the dog lay, calmer now, in the shade. I felt bad about what I was about to do, but I had no choice. There was no time to lose. I ran towards the stall, and as I ran, I roared. The poor dog saw me at once. It leapt to its feet. What it had of hair was standing on end. It began to bark. I ran round so that I was in front of it, and I urged it towards the car. The dog whined, tried to side step me, but I moved again, blocked its path. Everyone turned to look. The dog was jumping this way and that to get away from me, but I would not let it go. I spread my arms wide, I roared again and it whined and began to back away from me. Such was the commotion that the woman from the stall began running after it, shouting angrily, though I could not understand a word she said. Everyone was looking, and the dog went between barking and whining as it backed away from me. Its panic was catching. Other dogs joined in. And I knew they could see me too. I was ushering the dog toward Miss Baxter's car, relentless in my determination. This was the only way I could think of to stop him.

The man had already leapt to his feet. Barking dogs were everywhere in the square. I knew there had been no time for him to do anything. I saw people emerge from the church, Miss Baxter too, and I saw at once that she recognised this man. I could tell. Even from this distance I could see her eyes flash with recognition. He saw it too. He stumbled against the wall and almost fell over one of the dogs. Then he ran off into the crowds and was lost among them.

Miss Baxter raced down the steps of the church, she ran to her car, stopping almost beside me. So close I could have reached out and touched her.

She looked frightened. I stepped away from the poor dog. It had stopped barking, but it still shivered. I could see its bones quivering. The woman from the stall gripped its collar. She began ranting on in a foreign language. Miss Baxter leaned down and patted the dog's head.

' I think you saved my life, old friend,' she said.

The woman from the stall didn't understand. She only smiled and pulled the dog away. Miss Baxter stood for a moment. She thought she was alone. She thought no one could hear her whispered words.

' They know I'm after them.'

And that was the moment I knew why Miss Baxter had led me here. She knew I was ready to abandon her, she could not risk that. She wanted me to know she had not committed suicide. Nor had it been an accident that had killed her.

Miss Baxter had been murdered.

CHAPTER 16

And I had saved her ....hadn't I?

Of course I had. If I hadn't been here, that man would have finished what he was doing to her car. She would have come out of the church, and driven away, down that long, winding, dangerous road. She would have lost control of the car. It would have careered over the cliffs and into the sea. She would have died in that 'tragic accident'.

If I hadn't been there.

I had saved her. Wasn't this what she had been asking me to do, and *I* had done it?

I waited for the world to change the way it had before when I changed the past. When I had saved someone from an unlawful death. I waited for the wind to whip up, and the sky to spin. I waited, and nothing happened. And I wondered why?

I had saved her from dying. I had stopped it happening.

So why was nothing changing? I looked around. The people in the market still chose their wares. The dogs still barked. There was hardly a breeze. Certainly no tornado of changing time.

Instead, the sunny whitewashed village shimmered around me, the noises seemed to fade. The market, the people there, they all began to melt into the light. A coldness came over me. I blinked, and when I looked again. I was back in my home town, in the present. I was in the residents' car park behind the block of flats, heavy dark clouds hung low in the sky. The wind whipped up some papers lying on the ground sending them spinning and turning.

I was back.

A horn sounded behind me. Made me jump. There was a car trying to get into the car park. I was blocking its way. The driver waved me aside, her face filled with annoyance. I stumbled against the wall. She must have thought better of her bad temper when she saw that. She stopped beside me and her window slid down. 'You all right, dear?'

I was shaking. Still trying to take in what happened. ' I feel a bit sick.' That was no lie. I did feel sick. ' I want to go home.'

' Do you want a lift?'

I shook my head. ' No... I don't live far...and I think the walk will do me good.'

I took a deep breath and began walking. Miss Baxter had been murdered. That much I knew now. But I had saved her. Now , surely, she had to be alive and well, and living with her parents again in that little semidetached house. There was only one way for me to find out, to make sure. I knew I shouldn't, I had been warned to stay away, but I had no choice. I had to know. I began to hurry.

I was going back to her house .

I stood at the corner of Miss Baxter's street. From here I could see her parents' house. The windows were open, the curtains fluttered. I don't know how long I stood there, just watching. It took so much of my courage to walk down that street. I knew the welcome I would receive unless…..unless Miss Baxter hadn't died.   Unless she was indeed alive now. I would know as soon as that door was opened to me. If I was greeted with a smile…or even a questioning look. A ' who on earth are you, dear,' kind of look, I would know I had done it. I had saved her. She was alive.

And I must have saved her. I had stopped him from tampering with the car therefore the accident hadn't happened.

I pushed open the gate. It squeaked too loudly, and I hesitated, waiting for someone to have heard, to appear at a window. But there was nothing. Just a late summer evening kind of quiet. Even when I reached the door it took me a long moment to pluck up the courage to lift my hand and press the bell.

I could hear its ringing from inside the house, and then, footsteps coming down the hallway. My heart raced. My throat was as dry as dust.

Praying it was over. Praying everything had changed.

CHAPTER 17

I knew as soon as Mr. Baxter opened the door that I had changed nothing. His eyes flashed with anger as soon as he saw me. ' You again!'

I began to stammer. ' Please....'

' What the hell will it take to keep you away from here! A court order. Because I'll get it if I have to.'

He tried to push the door closed, but I wouldn't let him close the door on me. Even though I was mixed up and scared. I put my hand up to stop him, because even if he hated me, I had something important to tell him. If I hadn't managed to save her, then there had to be another reason that she had taken me back to that little village in Crete. She wanted me to let them know that their daughter had not committed suicide. She wanted them to know the truth.

' Mr. Baxter, your daughter didn't commit suicide. I know that as a fact. She didn't kill herself.'

I saw him grow angrier, his face flushed almost purple.

' Mr. Baxter are you listening! Don't ask me how I know, but I know. You have to get someone to look into her death.' I took a deep breath. ' Your daughter was murdered.'

He stepped back as if I had hit him with a brick. I thought at first he was going to collapse on the doorstep. The colour drained from his face. He looked back into the house as if he was afraid someone inside might hear me. Mrs. Baxter, the mother who had never got over her daughter's death. His voice grew soft, but the anger in it was just the same. ' Get away from this house. And don't come back.'

Why wouldn't he listen to me? I had told them, I could do no more. It was surely up to them now, to investigate her death. ' She was murdered, Mr. Baxter.' I said it one last time.

Did I say it too loudly? A sound almost like some kind of animal roar came from inside the house. I could see the silhouette of a woman heading like a demon towards me. Mr. Baxter turned his back on me, held his hands wide as if he was barring her way. ' She's going, love.' Then he looked back at me. 'Get away from here!'

But there was no time for me to run. I took one step back, but the woman was hurtling down the hallway. It was Mrs. Baxter. Nothing could stop her. She was like a roaring train heading my way. She was a big heavy woman, her hair wild and grey flying around her, a woman who had stopped taking any care of herself.

' What's she saying about our girl!' she was screaming. ' What's she saying!'

Mr. Baxter tried to hold her back, calm her down. He grabbed her shoulders, but there was a wildness in her he couldn't control. ' Don't listen to her. Go back inside. I'll handle this.'

I thought Mrs. Baxter would grab at me, drag me inside the house. I was so scared I froze to the spot. She shoved her husband aside, and she looked at me at last.

And she stopped yelling. She was in a single moment, silent. Her bloodshot eyes flamed even redder. She pulled herself away from her husband, moved towards me. I stepped back .

' You....' her voice trailed away. She began to shake her head. ' No...no...not possible....can't be possible...' There was a look on her face that for a moment I couldn't understand- then I saw what it was.

Terror. She looked terrified. Terrified of me?

Her mouth went slack. She began to crumple, and then she slipped to the floor.

Mr. Baxter stared at me. His eyes wild. ' What have you done? What have you done?"

And then I was frightened too. And I began to run.

CHAPTER 18

I didn't stop running. I didn't dare. Why had Mrs. Baxter looked at me like that? She had frightened me, yet I had frightened her too. And what did she mean...' not possible?'

Here again, when I had only wanted to do the right thing, everything had gone wrong. I had a feeling I was in even more trouble.

I didn't want to go home. I was too upset.

It was Jazz's house I went to. I needed to talk to someone. It was her mother who opened the door, a tall slim woman, with jet black hair, and long jangly earrings, and a spider web tattoo on her neck. I always felt this was exactly how Jazz would look when she was older.

She greeted me with a big smile. ' Oh hello, Tyler.' She must have seen then, by my face, that I had been running, my face streaked with tears. I must have looked like a wild woman myself. ' Is something wrong, Tyler?'

Jazz popped up behind her. ' Come on in, Tyler.' She nudged at her mum. ' Bet she's had an argument with Mac.'

Her mother nodded. That solution satisfied her. ' Oh come on, hen, don't worry about that.' She put an arm round my shoulders. Pulled me gently inside the house. ' See boys! More trouble than they're worth! Plenty more fish in the sea, that's what I say.'

Jazz led me up to her room. Not saying a word, until the door was safely closed behind us. ' Right! What's happened ? '

I burst into tears. ' I've just been to the Baxter's house, Jazz. I think I'm going to be in terrible trouble.'

' Why on earth did you go there?'

And what could I tell her? I couldn't tell her Miss Baxter had led me to Crete that afternoon, that I had been wandering about a foreign market, had seen a man tampering with her car.

' You've seen her again, haven't you?'

That was enough for her to know. I nodded. ' Miss Baxter didn't commit suicide, Jazz, I think she was murdered.'

Jazz's mouth hung open. For a moment she was lost for words. Not a natural state for Jazz. She threw herself back on the bed. She was loving this.

' Murdered? Who murdered her? And why would anyone want to murder a teacher...' she giggled. 'Hey, silly question. A teacher's the perfect target!'

I couldn't laugh with her. I was too upset.

'You have got to find out who did it.'

I know who did it, I wanted to tell her. But instead I said. ' No. I'm in enough trouble.' I covered my face with my hands. ' I went to their house to tell them, I thought it would be good for them to know, and Mrs. Baxter...she went crazy when she saw me.' I had a sudden flash of that look in her eyes again. Sheer terror. Why? I began to shiver.

'Was she drunk?'

I looked up at Jazz. ' Drunk?'

Jazz whispered. ' She's an alcoholic, didn't you know? They say she went back on the drink after that teacher of yours died. That was the ' psychiatric problems' they all talked about.' She sketched the inverted commas in the air. 'Was she drunk?' she asked again.

I thought back to that moment when she'd come at me, flying down the hall, her hair wild, her eyes bloodshot, and I knew Jazz was spot on, she had been drunk.

For a moment it made me feel better. That look, those words, had been brought on by alcohol. That was the answer.

She had been drunk.

' How do you know all these things, Jazz?'

She shrugged. ' I'm nosy, it runs in the family, my mum's nosy. She knows everything about everybody.'

Jazz was so excited. And I thought, not for the first time, that this gift I had been given- if it was a gift, and not a curse- it would have been so much better if it had been given to Jazz.

Why me?

One day, I was going to find that out.

' Anyway, the real question is...how do *you* know all these things?'

I shook my head. ' I...see dead people....' it was all I said. Enough for Jazz. 'I don't understand why.'

Jazz began to shake wildly with enjoyment. ' You see dead people! I love it! Psychic! I knew from the first day I saw you there was something special about you, Tyler.'

It was good to have someone to talk to about it. Jazz always made me feel better, talking things through with her made them clearer in my head. ' Maybe I've done enough now, Jazz. She wanted them to know she was murdered. That she didn't kill herself. Now they know, they can do something about it.'

That seemed sensible to Jazz too. ' They can go to the police. Get them to investigate. I can't see what else you can do.'

Just then a message came up on Jazz's mobile.

Her face crimsoned when she read it. Her eyes darted to me.

' What is it? ' I asked.

She looked as if she might not tell me, but after a moment she handed me the phone. I gasped when I saw the message.

TYLER LAWLESS IS WEIRD AND WICKED. PASS IT ON.

' Who sent you that?'

But before she even had a chance to answer, the phone rang again. It was Aisha.

' Have you had it too?' Jazz asked her.

I didn't need to hear her answer.

' Who's sending them?' Jazz asked.

I bet I knew that the answer to that too. Liz Cole. She'd used the same tactic before when I was in Grovepark, though she always denied it was her. Text messages to humiliate me sent around the school.

'How would she get our numbers?' Jazz said when I told her.

' Pass it on,' I said. ' Send it one person, and someone's bound to pass it on, and on...'

My stomach was sinking fast. Because if Jazz and Aisha had got this message, so had they all. Including Mac.

' Phone that Annabelle and ask her!' Jazz said. ' We're not letting her away with this!'

I shook my head. Annabelle would only deny it too. She'd say it couldn't be nice sweet, completely changed Liz, and I would look even worse.

Mac called soon after. He'd had one too.

' It's gone all round the school, Tyler.'

All round the school! A message saying I was weird and wicked, and there would be more. I'd been through all this before, and now it was starting again, and all thanks to Miss Baxter.

CHAPTER 19

I dreaded going to school next day. There would be whispers and giggles, just as there had been at Grovepark. Thank goodness I would at least have my friends around me.

There was a surprise waiting for me as I turned the corner towards the bus stop. Mr. Baxter was there.

He was huddled close against the bushes. He looked cold, or maybe he was just nervous. I stepped back, but he beckoned me over to him.

' I have to speak to you, Tyler,' he said. He knew my name. He must have been told it was me who had started the suicide story.

He kept glancing around as if he was afraid someone was watching us. It made me nervous too.

I found myself apologising again. ' I'm sorry if I upset your wife, Mr. Baxter. But I thought you would want to know....'

He held up his hand to stop me. His voice was low. I almost imagined someone listening somewhere behind the trees, head cocked, trying to catch his words. ' Don't say anything, Tyler. I shouldn't even be here. I came here to warn you. For your own good. Don't come back to our house, whatever you have on your mind, whatever you've found out, forget it, and don't come back.' He took a deep breath. His voice became even softer. ' It would be dangerous for you...and it would be dangerous for your family, for your friends.. for ...' he seemed to catch his breath. ' dangerous for.. us. Leave it be. Please.'

I was completely astounded. ' Dangerous? How do you mean, dangerous?'

He put his fingers to his lips. He kept shaking his head. ' Ssh, not so loud. I shouldn't even be here. I'm taking a terrible risk to tell you this. But you're only a girl. I have to warn you. Leave us alone. You don't know what you're getting into.'

' I don't understand. Your daughter was murdered, don't you care?'

He almost panicked when I said that. ' SShh! No. No. She wasn't murdered. You're wrong.' He said it as if he was trying to convince himself. Yet, I could see he knew she had been murdered. He believed me. Deep down it was what he had always suspected, yet he preferred the lie, the rumour that she had killed herself to the truth. Why? So many whys?

He was already moving away from me. He had said all he had come to say. But I wasn't finished with him.

' Why did I scare your wife so much?'

He swung round to me. He was breathing hard. He looked older. He seemed to age with every day I saw him. ' My wife's ill,' he said. ' She's been ill for a long time. She imagines things. That's why you have to let this go. She can't take much more.'

' What are not telling me? Why am I in danger? Are the people who murdered your daughter, after you too. Are they after me?'

I had hit the truth. He was suddenly shouting at me. ' Leave us be! I've warned you. If you care about your family, if you care about your friends, leave this be! I won't be responsible for what happens to you after this. Do you hear me?'

He stumbled away, and I stood for a moment and wondered. Why was I in danger? Had the man who had killed Miss Baxter come here? Was he in this town? Was he watching me? That tall dark man with the scar who had tampered with her car that day in Crete? What exactly had Miss Baxter stumbled into?

I looked around, sure I could feel that scarred man's eyes burning into me. More afraid than I had ever been.

CHAPTER 20

School was every bit as bad as I expected it to be. Whispers and innuendos followed me everywhere. I hardly listened at any of the lessons. All I wanted to do was to go home. Mr. Clisham's class was the last of the day, and I hardly heard a word he said. Not until he shouted. ' Tyler Lawless! Am I so boring!'

I jumped in my seat. " Yes, sir.' There was a ripple of giggles. '...I mean, no sir?'

' Any idea what I might have been talking about?'

Mr. Clisham strolled up the aisle to my desk. I swallowed. Mac was behind him, mouthing something to me. I tried desperately to make it out. 'Battlecries?' I said hopefully.

Everyone laughed. Mac rolled his eyes.

' You were close,' the teacher said. He turned to the class. ' Anyone like to inform Tyler what the subject was?'

Callum was the first to speak. 'It was really interesting ,sir. You were talking about the butterfly effect.'

The butterfly effect? Most of the class were noddng, they all seemed to agree with Callum. It was really interesting. Butterflies? They were hooked on butterflies?

Callum looked at me. ' It's really fascinating, Tyler. You should listen. '

Mr. Clisham looked smug. It wasn't often anyone found his lessons interesting, let alone fascinating. 'The butterfly effect. It's a theory a man called Lorenz came up with. The idea that the fluttering of a butterfly's wings in Brazil, could cause a tornado in Texas. That one small thing can have a major effect on everything else. '

Adam called out. ' But sir, you were talking about how fiction writers grabbed the idea, the idea that one tiny thing you might change in the past, could change the future forever in ways you couldn't understand.'

Change the past, and change the future? Now, I was alert. ' Wouldn't that be a good thing? If you could stop something terrible from happening? If you could save someone's life in the past?'

He turned to me. ' You might think so, but, if you look at it in another way, Tyler, changing something in the past is not always a good thing. What if Hitler had been meant to die in the first World War, and you pushed him clear of the bullet that should have killed him? You saved his life. But if he had died, there would have been no Second World War, and millions upon millions of people would have lived.'

' Big mistake!' Callum shouted.

Mr. Clisham went on. ' You see, you don't know what harm you might be doing by changing the past. Even on a smaller scale changing one small thing can change everything. Okay, have you ever heard your mum or dad say they wanted to go somewhere, or be something, but for one reason or another they didn't?'

I didn't even have to think about it. ' My mum was supposed to go to America when she was eighteen. She was going to live with my Aunt Belle out there. But my granddad had an accident in the shipyards, and she stayed to help my gran look after him, and then she met my dad and she never went...she's always talking about what her life might have been like if she'd gone.'

He sat on the desk. ' Okay,' he looked round the class. " Can anyone tell me what would have happened if Tyler had gone back in time, and stopped her grandfather having that accident, and her mother *had* gone to America? '

Hands shot up all over the room.

' Tyler's mum wouldn't have met her dad. She'd have married someone else.'

' Tyler would be at school in America now.'

' Don't be daft.' Callum said. ' Tyler would never have been born.'

I drew in my breath. I would never have been born. I would not even exist.

Mr. Clisham nodded. 'Exactly. Tyler would never have been born. She wouldn't be in this school, she wouldn't have met all of you. And Mac would possible pay more attention at lessons if she wasn't here.'

I blushed, but only for a moment. I had to know more. ' But what if you went back and stopped someone good from being killed, how could that be bad?'

' Oh gosh, she's writing another story, sir!' Adam yelled.

' I remember reading a story once…' this was Callum. ' It was about an American president, a really good man, and someone finds out he's going to be assassinated, and they stop it. The president lives…and he goes on to start the third world war and it turns out that the man who was going to assassinate him had come back from the future because he knew that the only way to save the world was to kill that President.'

' Hey, Terminator, movie, same thing!' Adam, our movie expert, yelled out.

' Never a good thing to tamper with the past, sir,' Callum decided.

It started a heated debate in the class, about time slip movies and stories about changing the past, and all I could do was think, was I meant to hear this? Was this to tell me I should stop now, change nothing else in time? I had not stopped Miss Baxter dying. Perhaps I wasn't meant to. Perhaps this explained the dream I had, the warning not to help her. Warning me not to change her past.

What right had I to do that anyway?

' Luckily,' Mr. Clisham went on, the lesson was almost ended. ' it is impossible to go back in time. No matter what Einstein says. So we never have to worry about it.'

Callum whispered as we left the class. ' And of course, what would Einstein know? He was only a genius.'

Everyone laughed. They were all still talking about the lesson. But I wasn't laughing. Because I *could* go back in time. I could change things. I *had* changed things.

But maybe, just maybe, I wasn't meant to do this. I had done as much as I was able. I had found out Miss Baxter was murdered. It was up to the Baxters to do the rest.

CHAPTER 21

There were more giggles about me as I left the school that day. I knew even more texts had come through that I didn't know about. I felt miserable. My bus came, and just as I was about to step inside, I saw her. Miss Baxter, inside waiting for me. She looked paler, more like a ghost than she ever had. She stared at me, and she looked angry. I held back.

' Come on, hen, you're holding up the queue,' the driver said. The woman behind tried to push me forward.

For the first time I was afraid of Miss Baxter. I stepped back onto the street. The people behind me filed onto the bus. I stood and watched her, waiting for her to float toward me. She didn't move, but she never took her dark eyes off me.

I began to run.

It took me a long time to get home. I kept watching for her, thinking I was going to see her again, in a crowd, as I turned a corner, waiting for me at another bus stop. All the way home, I could think of nothing else. Why was she back? What else did she expect me to do?

The house was empty when I rushed in. Mum and dad at work, Steven too. I was alone.

But not for long.

I opened the door of the living room, and there she was, standing by the window. She had dark circles under her eyes. She looked almost transparent. Her hands reached out to me.

' Help me.'

I shouted at her. ' I've done all I can!'

She began to shake her head. ' Help me, ' she said again.

' Why me? Why has it got to be me!' I didn't want it to be me.

' We all wait for you. We all need you....' Her voice seemed to come from a dark place and as she spoke, figures formed behind her. Ghostly, silent figures, and all of them reaching out to me. ' Only you can help us, Tyler. Only you.'

Only me.

The figures faded. Miss Baxter stepped closer.

' I don't know what else I can do. Tell me!' I said.

Yet I knew, almost as if she *was* telling me, but not with words, with feelings. She had struggled to stay here, to ask for my help.

And in the same moment I knew why she was so pale. She was losing that power. The longer it took for me to help her, the less chance she had of staying. Time was running out.

She came closer. ' Help...help them.' That's what she said. ' Help them.'

' Them? Who is them?'

' The children,' she said, her voice less than a whisper. ' The children need you.' And then she was gone, like smoke disappearing in the air.

Help the children? What was she talking about? And yet, something was niggling at the back of my mind. That day at the library, she had been pointing to the paper. I thought she meant there was something in that paper about her death.... was she, instead, pointing at the headline? The one about the little boy who had been snatched? There was something else in my memory, something I couldn't quite grasp. I ran upstairs to my laptop, and switched it on.

I punched in the date when I had first seen her. How could I forget it? It had been almost Christmas, busy shops, bright lights.

And there it was, the headline I was almost sure I would find.

WHERE IS MOLLY?

A little girl gone missing.

A family were on a day out at a Christmas market, one minute little Molly Gerber was on the roundabout, and when it stopped the mother ran round to get her, and she was gone. The parents were distraught, begging whoever had taken her to bring her back. Little Molly Gerber had been gone for a week when Miss Baxter first appeared to me.

When exactly had I begun to see Miss Baxter? Five days ago.

My fingers shook as I clicked into the story that was the headlines now.

The little boy who had been snatched from the park. Still the main headline in all the papers. Too much of a coincidence.

' Help the children,' Miss Baxter had said. Miss Baxter knew what was happening to those children. She wanted me to find out too.

CHAPTER 22

I had found a link at last. What had Miss Baxter to do with these missing children? And what had they to do with Crete? She had found out something about them when she was here. And that information had led her to Crete.

I knew now that I could not let this thing go. Like stepping on to a plane, once that plane takes off, you have no choice but to stay on board until it landed. I was on a journey with Miss Baxter.

Maybe she had been meant to die, and I couldn't change that. What I was meant to do was find those missing children.

No matter how I might try to avoid it, I knew I had to speak to Mr. Baxter whether he liked it or not. I had to find out how much they knew about her death and these missing children. I tried to find their phone number but they were obviously ex directory.

I had no choice. This time, I wouldn't go to his house. I wasn't going to break that promise. I'd go to the place where he worked.

Next morning, I didn't go to school. I left the house at the time I usually did to catch the bus, but instead of heading for the bus stop, I made my way across town and caught the bus on the main road to the gardening centre where I knew he worked.

It still hadn't opened when I got there. Set in an idyllic spot right on the river, the gardening centre had begun very small, a place for gardeners to go and pick up bedding plants and seeds and it had gradually grown, just like one of those seeds into almost a small village, with craft shops and furniture shops , and restaurants. I stood hidden in the trees across from the entrance, waiting for him to arrive.

I recognised his car as it came round the corner. I stepped even further back into the trees so he wouldn't see me. Invisible as I watched him drive past. He looked so old. His face drawn and grey. I was only making things worse for him, but in the end, I thought, I was going to make it better, wasn't I?

The butterfly effect. The teacher's lesson came back to me. Perhaps I was setting in motion a tornado that I could not control.

I waited till more people started to arrive. A trickle of early morning shoppers, retired couples, mothers with toddlers. As I walked in, I knew I looked out of place. A young girl in a school uniform, her bag slung over her shoulder.

The garden centre was huge, with long avenues of plants and shrubs. This was where I saw him, bending over some bedding plants, wearing a green overall with the garden centre logo on the pocket.

I could feel my heart thumping in my chest as I came up behind him. I touched his shoulder. He turned with a ready smile, to greet a customer, and saw me instead and the smile vanished.

' Have you not listened to a word I've said!' I'd never understood the term, through gritted teeth till that moment.

' I don't want to hurt anybody, Mr. Baxter. ' I touched his arm, didn't want him storming away from me. ' I have to know if your daughter's death had anything to do with these children who went missing.'

As soon as I said it, I knew that he knew it was true. His face turned waxen white. 'How do you...how can you...?' He looked all around, as if someone might be watching. He pulled me behind some bushes.

' I'm right, so I am? She went to Crete, and it had something to do with children going missing. She found something out there.'

He glanced around, as if he was fearful someone might be watching, listening. ' Leave it be! You're putting yourself in danger. You're putting all of us in danger. Leave it be!'

He was squeezing my arm so tight it hurt.

' Why don't you go to the police!' I said. ' I can give a description of the man who killed her.'

He seemed to panic then, waving his arms about him. ' How...how can you possibly know that?'

' We could go to the police together.'

' Let it rest!'

' There's another child gone missing, did you know that? A little boy has gone missing.'

In front of my eyes he seemed to shrink into his clothes. He shook his head. Staggered back. ' You think we don't know that? Nothing to do with us... get out of here....' He fell back against a wall. I reached out to catch him, but he pushed my hand away. ' You are putting yourself in danger. If you tell anyone about this, you put them in danger too. Can you get that through your head? Now get away from me.'

One of the other men ran to him, caught him before he fell. 'What happened?' He looked at me. 'What did you say to him?'

Another man came hurrying up. A big man, his biceps bulged from his rolled up sleeves. ' Out!' he said to me. ' I see you in here again and I'll have the cops on you.'

I stepped away, but before I left I spoke once more to Mr. Baxter. ' I won't let it rest. I can't. And one day, you're going to be grateful that I didn't!'

CHAPTER 23

It began to rain as I hurried from the Garden centre. A heavy summer shower, people ran sheltering from the downpour. I did too. I stopped under the trees till it went off. Rain dripped from the leaves onto my head. I was shivering, but it wasn't from the cold. I was getting myself into more trouble, and didn't know how to stop. I was in danger? I was putting my friends in danger?

How could that be? Then I remembered the scarred man I had seen at Miss Baxter's car. He had killed Miss Baxter, I was sure of that. Perhaps he was here now, watching me.

I jumped when my phone in my pocket rang. It was Jazz.

' Where are you? How are you not at school? Are you sick?'

I didn't want to start explaining, so I told a silly lie. ' Yeah, I'm in bed.'

A lorry roared past just then, splashing me.

' Where's your bed? In the middle of the road?' Jazz sounded uncharacteristically annoyed. 'Where are you!' This time not a question. A demand. ' We're supposed to be meeting up later, organise everything for Mac's party! Are you not interested? You've done nothing to help. What's wrong, Tyler?'

I had forgotten. I was always forgetting. ' I'll call you later,' all I said, then I snapped down the phone. Too mixed up to talk. Trying to work things out in my head. Home, I decided. I would go home, tell my mum I felt sick, hope the police didn't turn up at our door. But they wouldn't. Mr. Baxter would not let them know I had been to see him. I'd go home and say I felt sick. Not a lie. I did feel sick, sick and tired.

The downpour turned to a drizzle, and I left my shelter and ran for the bus stop. There was already a long queue there, and lorries, cars and buses roared up and down the busy coast road.

I stepped onto the pavement and knocked against a woman and she turned and scowled at me.

' Sorry,' I said, and moved back, and managed to step on someone else's toes. ' Sorry,' I said again, as I turned to apologise.

The boy behind me shrugged. He was on his mobile phone, chewing gum. He had dark blue eyes, and he made a face at the woman who had scowled . He closed over his mobile and he winked at me with those dark blue eyes. I smiled back, and moved to the back of the queue.

And there , standing at the other end, right at the front of the queue, was Anne and her mother.

Her face beamed with pleasure when she spotted me. She came skipping up to me. ' I knew I'd see you again. Where are you going?'

She didn't wait for an answer. Anne pulled at my arm. ' Come and stand with us. ' she said.

' I think people might be a bit annoyed if I jump the queue.'

' I'll tell them you're my sister,' she said, all smiles, and I remembered the sister who died. She looked around. ' Not a soul's looking at us. They'll not even notice.' She pulled at me again. ' Come on, I want my mum to see you.'

I thought I would be the last person her mother would want to see. ' You better go back, Anne. The bus will be coming soon.'

Her lips curled into a pout. ' I'm only trying to be nice,' she said.

' I know, but I can't just go to the front of the queue.'

She didn't look convinced. She sucked in her cheeks. She looked annoyed, and I could see her mother in her then. She stamped her feet. ' Why does nobody ever do what I want!' She turned and stomped back to her mother.

Here was another mystery. What had Anne to do with all this? I was meant to do something for her, perhaps something to do with her dead sister, I was sure of it, but I couldn't think of it now. One thing at a time, I prayed to the unlawful dead. I can only handle one thing at a time. This one thing was exhausting me. Please, only one thing at a time.

A bus appeared round the corner, just visible behind an articulated truck roaring down the road. People began to shuffle forward, ready to file onto the bus.

And that's when it happened. One minute I was moving forward with everyone else- and the next, I felt hands on my back. I was pitched forward. I couldn't keep my feet. I heard someone screaming. It might have been me. I was tumbling forward and falling right in the path of that huge truck.

CHAPTER 24

I was going to die. In that moment I knew it. I was going to join the unlawfully dead. Become one of them myself. All I could see were the headlights of that truck as it thundered towards me, blasting its horn, the driver's face terrified as he braked, twisting the wheel to avoid me. I could see, was sure I could see the veins bulging in his head as he tried desperately to stop his truck before it hit me. Yet, I felt as if I was moving in slow motion, falling forward, my hands reaching out trying to grab at something to pull myself out of the path of that truck. I saw the people at the bus stop, the scowling woman, the blue eyed boy, horrified, shocked, reaching out to me, but no one could help me. It was too late.

And then, blackness closed in.

I opened my eyes, and a man was leaning over me. An angel? He smiled and looked even more like an angel to me. 'You're awake. Good.'

Not an angel. He was a paramedic. I was alive. A wave of nausea swept over me and I had to force myself not to vomit all over him.

' The truck...' It seemed as if my voice echoed, as if I was in a tunnel.

' The truck's fine,' the paramedic said cheerfully. ' Not a scratch on it . And you're going to be fine too. It stopped just in time.'

I could see curious, concerned faces all around me. I tried to get to my feet. The paramedic held me down. ' Oh no, you don't. We're taking you to the hospital. Get you checked out. You banged your head when you fell.'

I wanted to tell him someone had pushed me. But my tongue seemed too big for my mouth, my lips stuck together. My eyes moved behind the paramedic to the crowd. Someone there had pushed me, someone looking at me now, had pushed me into the path of that truck.

I looked around again as I was being helped into the ambulance. And suddenly it wasn't who was there I was looking for, but who wasn't there.

Anne, the little girl, was nowhere in sight. Me, the ' friend' she was so fond of had almost been run over, and she hadn't waited around to see how I was? The bus was still there at the bus stop, lying idle behind the truck, passengers craning their necks for a look at me. Was she on that bus? Or... where had she gone?

The journey to the hospital was a blur of faces and voices. Everyone was very kind, and thoughtful, but there was something in their eyes, that bothered me. And it wasn't concern for my health.

I was to be kept in overnight for observation. I didn't want to stay. I wanted home. And apart from a dull headache, I felt fine.

I was put in a four bed ward with three older women. The woman in the bed across from me came over almost as soon as I was left alone. She dragged her drip along with her.

' I'm Tilly, darling. What on earth happened to you?'

She had long strands of blonde hair, curled on her shoulders. Her face was lined and chubby and cheerful. ' I...' I wanted to say I was pushed...but stopped myself. ' I was almost hit by a truck.'

She smiled. ' My goodness that could be nasty.' She rubbed my arm. ' But you look fine.'

She fussed around me for a moment before she trailed her drip back and climbed into her own bed.

Mum and dad came rushing in, no hiding how worried they were. ' What on earth were you doing outside that garden centre?' Dad asked.

' Why didn't you go to school?' Mum's question.

I had known these would be the first things they wanted to know. ' Someone pushed me.' I said, the first time I had spoken it aloud.

Mum's eyes flashed. ' Someone pushed you!' She sounded relieved. Why would she be relieved at such a terrible thing? ' You mean, accidentally?'

' That's not what we were told.' Dad's voice came out cold.

' What were you told?'

Mum sat on the bed. She took my hand. ' The people at the bus stop said it looked as if...'

' As if someone pushed me!' I finished it for her.

' No Tyler,' Dad said, his voice cold. ' They said it looked as if you threw yourself in front of that truck.'

I leapt up on the bed. Shouted though I didn't mean to. ' I threw myself?' I looked from her to dad. 'You don't really believe I would do that?'

Mum shook her head assured me she didn't. ' No, of course not...'

At the same time dad was saying. ' You've been behaving very strangely the last few days, Tyler. All this carryon with the Baxters...and these text messages, we've heard about them too.....is there something you're not telling us?'

I wanted to scream at him. 'Yes, there's lots I'm not telling you! ' But of course I said nothing.

He drew a chair close to the bed and sat down. ' Where did you go today? And why were you at that bus stop anyway?'

The words tumbled out before I could stop them. ' I went to see Mr. Baxter, he said I was in danger, I had to know...'

I didn't get it finished. Dad's face went purple with anger. ' You went to see that man! You promised this business was over!' He drew his hands through his hair in anger. ' Tyler...what are you doing to us!'

I sat forward, reached for his hand. He drew it away from me. ' Don't you see, dad, Mr. Baxter said I was in danger, and he was right, someone pushed me under that truck!'

He held up his hands. ' Someone pushed you. I've never heard such nonsense! I don't believe that for a minute.'

' You'd rather think I jumped. Is that it?'

Mum put her hands to her face, tears trickling through her fingers. I didn't want to make my mum cry. Neither did Dad. ' You'll be getting out tomorrow,' he said. ' We'll talk then. I'm just asking you one thing...please don't go on about someone pushing you. It'll only get them asking questions in here. Just say you tripped. Will you?'

They didn't believe it. They didn't want to believe it.

They left after that and I was glad to see them go. I lay back in the bed. Had it really looked as if I had jumped? But someone *had* pushed me. I could still almost feel the hands on my back. Feel the shove that sent me sprawling forward.

An image of the scarred man came to me. He had tried to kill Miss Baxter. Was he here now, and after me?

And if he tried once, wouldn't he try again? I was in danger. And according to Mr. Baxter, so perhaps were my family, my friends. I had confided only in Jazz. Had I put her in danger too?

CHAPTER 25

I tried to rest, but I couldn't . My mind was too full for any kind of sleep. Going over and over what had happened. Whoever had pushed me had been in that queue. I had seen them. I tried to remember if perhaps I had seen the scarred man without realising it. Perhaps he had slipped into the queue without me seeing him. But there was only one face that kept swimming into view. It was Anne's. All smiles at first, then annoyed because I wouldn't go to the front of the queue with her. Stamping her feet because she wasn't getting her own way. And in my mind's eye, that little annoyed face morphed into something sinister. She had been the last face I'd seen before I turned away to look for the bus. Before I saw that powerful truck ploughing down the street. Before I felt the hands on my back.

I began to sweat. Who was she? Who was this Anne?

My friends arrived in force at visiting time. I was so glad to see them, and blushed to remember how I'd snapped the phone shut while Jazz was still talking. I almost felt like crying. Felt the tears well up in my eyes, but I blinked them back. Jazz and Aisha ran to each side f my bed and hugged me.

' What happened? ' Aisha said. ' Why weren't you at school?'

I longed to tell them all the truth. Share the story. But I was afraid now, that any hint that they knew what I knew would put them in harm's way.

I shook my head. ' I had to do something... for mum.' It sounded like the lie it was. And Mac looked puzzled, they all did.

Adam grinned. 'Wish my mum would give me something to do so I could miss school.'

Callum laughed too. ' Don't suppose you'll be back to school tomorrow either, eh? Two days off, lucky devil.'

Jazz sat on the bed beside me. ' Hey, I think I'll throw myself under a bus and get a couple of days off school. '

I shouted so loud everyone else in the ward turned to face us. ' I didn't throw myself under that truck. And don't you dare say I did!'

Jazz stood up. She looked stunned. ' It was a joke, Tyler... I didn't mean.....'

But it was Mac's reaction that hurt the most. ' For goodness sake, Tyler, what are you acting like this for? We're your friends. You've been dead funny lately. What's your problem?'

I wanted to say, sorry. I wanted to explain, couldn't say a word. It was Aisha who took charge. 'Tyler's been through a lot today. I think we should just leave her to rest.'

Jazz sat back on the bed. She took my hand. She could never stay annoyed for long. ' I think you should tell them, Tyler. We're all your friends. We won't think you're weird. You need people to know what's going on.'

And before I could stop her she just rattled on. ' Tyler has a gift. She can see ghosts. And she's been seeing that old teacher again. And that teacher told her she hadn't died in an accident. She'd been murdered. Can you blame her for acting funny with all that going on? That's what's wrong with her.' She smiled at me, as is she had made it better. 'Isn't it, Tyler?'

I hesitated for a moment, just looking at her.

Tell the truth and she's in danger. Tell the truth and they're all in danger. I couldn't risk putting my friends in danger. I shook my head. ' You really are making me sound weird, Jazz. You didn't really believe that, did you?' I looked around them. ' I'm writing a story. I knew Jazz would be the only one who'd take it in. I wanted her reaction.'

Jazz looked puzzled and then hurt. She drew her hand away. ' A story? You made that whole thing up? To make me look like a mug? What kind of person are you, Tyler? '

' That was a bit cruel, Tyler,' Aisha said.

' Can you not take a joke?' I tried to say it lightly.

' I don't think that was much of a joke, Tyler,' Aisha said.

Jazz turned away. ' Some friend you are.' I was sure she wanted to say more, would have said more if she hadn't been in a hospital. 'I think I'm going.'

Aisha followed her.

I looked at Mac. ' I didn't mean to hurt anybody. '

I hoped he might stay and talk, but he didn't. When Adam and Callum silently followed the girls, Mac only nodded grimly and went after them. I had never felt so completely alone. But what else could I have done?

CHAPTER 26

A hospital is an eerie place at night time. I woke up, and it was dark. The curtains were drawn, but there was a line of light coming from between the blinds leading out to the silent corridors. The other three women in the ward slept peacefully. The ward was in darkness, but a green light beeped at regular intervals from the machine at the bed opposite me, Tilly's bed. The woman in the bed beside mine snored gently . I wanted to go back to sleep, my head ached, but I couldn't bear asking for aspirin to dull the pain.

I closed my eyes, and opened them almost immediately. A movement caught my eye in the shadowy corner of the ward.

I looked above the covers. I peered into the darkness. Another movement and I knew then what had awoken me. Her presence. Miss Baxter was here.

She seemed to glide from the shadows toward me. Her eyes didn't leave mine. Those eyes with the dark circles all around them. I could almost see through her, it was as if she was fading in front of me. As she came closer she beckoned me to follow her. The door of the ward opened. Just like that. It simply opened .

I slipped from the bed. No sound of my bare feet on the floor. Part of me was thinking....this is a dream. This isn't really happening. I was moving so silently behind her.

I stepped through the door of the ward, but I didn't step into the hospital corridor. I was somewhere else entirely. It was still night outside. The sky through the window was black with stars. I knew at once where I was. Back in Crete.

I could tell by the sudden heat that enveloped me, continental heat. I could tell by the smell of jasmine from the open window, the sound of crickets in the night air. I was still in a corridor, but it looked more like the hallway of some old house. Brick walls, tiled floor. Miss Baxter, the real, alive Miss Baxter, was in front of me. She was wearing a light summer dress, moving forward down a dark hallway, her hands pressed against the wall. Sneaking. The only word to describe what she was doing.

I could hear the soft murmur of voices from somewhere in front of us. Miss Baxter heard it too. She stopped, listened. There was light coming from an open door ahead of her. I couldn't make out what was being said, and neither, it seemed could Miss Baxter. She moved closer, and so did I. So close I was sure she could feel my breath against her neck. She was straining to hear. I moved past her and into that room.

There were two men and a woman sitting round a table, papers spread out in front of them. They couldn't see me. They never even looked up as I moved closer. I was an invisible ghost to them. They were speaking in a foreign language. One of them thumped the desk. They were angry. The older man lifted his phone, punched in a number. When he spoke it was in English. ' Rick, when will the merchandise be ready? We have a buyer.'

The man relayed the answer to the other two. ' It's on its way,' he smiled.

There was a sudden commotion in the corridor. I heard a cry, and something slumped to the floor. Then a man appeared, pushing his way into the room, and I recognised him right away. It was the scarred man .He looked furious. The scar on his face was white, livid with rage.

' She heard everything!'

The others jumped to their feet. They moved past me. Miss Baxter was lying unconscious on the tiled floor.

' We have to get rid of her.' The scarred man said, as if he was talking of taking out the rubbish.

He lifted her in his arms. I heard her moan. Her body flopped against him. She was alive at least. I moved towards her. ' Miss Baxter,' I whispered it, but of course she couldn't hear me. I reached out to touch her, but I wasn't solid. I wasn't real. I was in her time. I was a ghost.

' Leave her be!' I yelled it out, and the door of the office banged shut.

It didn't stop them. Already Miss Baxter was being carried out. I followed them.

Her car was parked in an alley behind the building. That same little yellow car she had had at the market. The man had obviously found it, and knew she was here. They hardly had to speak, their decision about her fate already decided. He laid Miss Baxter in the front seat, then he slid in behind the wheel. Without even opening the door, without even thinking about it, I was in the car with them.

He shouted something to the others, and then he drove off.

I had to be dreaming. I prayed so hard I was dreaming.

He began to drive, faster and faster, his face stern and angry. Up the long narrow twisting road, higher and higher up the mountain. Even though I knew I was in no danger, not here, no one could hurt *me here,* I was afraid. The car tossed this way and that, tipping on the edge of the mountain road. It was pitch black, with only the beam of his headlights lighting the way ahead of us. Blackness on either side of us.

This was how she had died. I had indeed stopped the tampering earlier, but she hadn't been meant to die then. This was the moment, the real moment of her death. Her car had gone careering off a cliff. This was the 'accident' that had killed her. It was about to happen, it was now I was meant to stop it. To save her. And the only way I could do that was by reaching him.

I tried to touch his face, to scare him. But he brushed my fingers away, as if they were a moth touching his skin. I screamed at him. How could he not hear my voice, but it was travelling through time. Too far away for him to hear.

The car screeched to a stop. This was the place. A sharp bend in the road, easy to lose control of a car there, especially a car travelling too fast. He stepped out and pulled

113

Miss Baxter into the driving seat. She moaned a little, but she was still unconscious. I was shaking now. I didn't know what to do. I couldn't make him see me. I couldn't wake Miss Baxter up. How could I stop this!

I leapt from the car, tried to pull Miss Baxter free, my hands sunk into her as if I was smoke. She never stirred. The man was beside me. He leaned into the car and began turning the wheel, pushing the car forward, closer to the edge.

' Leave her be!' I screamed at him. Other people had seen me at moments like this. Why not him! Why couldn't I stop this!

This couldn't be happening. I was meant to stop her from dying. So why couldn't I do anything to help Miss Baxter now?

One more second and it would be too late. I had to do something. I screamed again. I banged at the car, and for a split second, I thought I had him. He looked around, as if he had heard something. I yelled again, banged even harder on the bonnet, but it was too late. I could see it was too late. There was no stopping the car now. It was too close to the edge of the cliff. The wheel tipped, the car followed, and I could do nothing to stop it.

Nothing.

Only watch as the car tumbled and crashed down to the sea. Over and over, breaking apart as it fell until it exploded in an angry flash of red and orange.

Miss Baxter was dead again.

CHAPTER 27

It wasn't meant to happen like this. I was meant to save her. Yet her car had careered down the cliff face, bursting into flames. This was not supposed to happen!

The scarred man stood close to me, watching the flames, his face impassive. I reached out to touch him, my hands passed through him. Yet he felt me. I know he did, for his fingers rubbed at the place where I had touched and he brushed at it, as if brushing away a fly.

We both turned as another car came up the road, its headlights sending a beam of light across the trees. My heart leapt. A witness, someone who could see what he had done. But the car slowed and the man headed for it. It was his accomplices. They had known where he would take her. They had followed him.

The door of the car swung open. It didn't even stop. They were leaving and I was lost. Lost and angry. I yelled, and my voice seemed to echo down, down to the sea. ' I'll get you for this. You'll pay, I promise!'

He stopped. He seemed to look right at me. I ran to him, and yelled again. ' It's me. Tyler Lawless! And I am coming for you. I'm coming for all of you.'

But he only turned from me and slipped inside the car. I could do nothing but watch it head back down the cliff road.

I was lost, didn't know what to do, and I didn't know how to get back to my own time. More afraid than I had ever been because I had failed. I walked back to the very edge of the cliff. The sea rushed in. The fire still burned. White tipped waves would soon smother the flames. I had let her down. After all this, I had let her down.

' Tyler.'

The voice came from close behind me, yet seemed so far away, almost a whisper of a voice.

It came again. ' Tyler! Step away from the edge.'

I blinked. A sudden cold wind made me shiver and in that second I knew I was no longer in Crete. I was back.

I opened my eyes, and looked down, and I began to panic.

I was standing on the edge of the hospital roof, looking down to the car park far below.

CHAPTER 28

' Step back from the edge.' The voice behind me was trying to sound calm, but there was fear in it too. ' One step at a time.'

I tried, but my feet wouldn't move for me. I was frozen to the spot. I began to feel dizzy, felt myself begin to sway back and forth, back and forth. And then, just when I thought I would surely fall, I was grabbed from behind, arms were wrapped around me tightly, and I was dragged to safety.

Two nurses held me. ' How on earth did you get up here!' one of them said.

I was shaking, panic setting in now.   Couldn't speak even if I wanted to.

They began to help me back to the stairs, talking about me as if I couldn't hear them.

' How did she manage to get past the night staff. Not a soul saw her. It was as if she was a ghost.'

My bare feet were filthy and scratched, and there were questions in all of their eyes. How had I managed to get to the roof unseen? And what was I doing there? The questions were there, but they didn't ask them that night. The questions could wait till the morning. They helped me into bed, tried to give me something to help me sleep, but I wouldn't take it. I would be fine I told them. And when I closed my eyes, I was asleep in seconds.

No dreams. To my surprise I had no dreams at all. As if my subconscious was telling me I could have done nothing else. Forget it. Put it behind you. If only.

But if I thought my ordeal was over I was wrong. In the morning, almost as soon as breakfast was over, a counsellor came into the ward. Or a psychologist, I don't know which. She pulled the curtains round my bed, and I could see Tilly across from me crane her neck to try to see what was happening. She winked at me, and it gave me some comfort.

' Please call me Jane,' the counsellor/psychologist told me. Trying to be my friend. I was on my guard as soon as she said it. ' We're trying to understand why you went up to the roof last night, Tyler,'

I had an answer for that, knew it would be the first question they would ask. ' I must have been sleepwalking.'

She lifted an eyebrow and nodded, one of those nods that says...'oh yes, we're supposed to believe that, are we?'

' Now here is the problem we've got, Tyler. Yesterday, you insisted someone had pushed you in front of that truck.' She held up a hand as if I had protested, when actually I hadn't said a word. ' Other witnesses said that you leapt in front of that truck.' And this time I did protest.

' That's a lie! They're wrong...'

She interrupted me, no, she ignored me more like.

' Last night you were found at the edge of the hospital roof. The nurses say you looked as if you were about to jump. Again.'

I tried to sound calm. ' No, I wasn't, I was sleepwalking, I don't know how I got up there. Honest.'

' You've been having some problems before you came into hospital, haven't you? Problems with some family, I believe. Now, I want to help you, Tyler. Is there any reason you have for behaving like this...?'

I knew what she was thinking. I was an attention seeker, I was a troublemaker. I was having problems at home. I took a deep breath before I answered her.

' I must have been wrong about someone trying to push me, I just stumbled, but I didn't jump. I'd never do that.' What was the point of telling anyone the truth anyway? No one believed me. ' I had a bump on the head, concussion, that must be the reason I was sleepwalking. I can't remember going up to the roof. I'm sorry if I've caused you all any problems.' I sounded logical and sensible, and I finished with a smile.

It wasn't enough for Jane. She still looked suspicious. ' You did leave your last school under a cloud, didn't you?'

She'd done her homework. She knew all about Miss Baxter.

She left, finally, with a promise that she was there for me if I needed her. As soon as she'd gone, Tilly slipped from her bed and, dragging her drip along with her, she crossed to mine. ' She's a nosy so and so,' she said. 'She came to me my first day here and said, 'do you know who I am?' And I said to her.' If you cannae remember who you are, hen, just ask the nurse, she'll tell you.' '

It was an old joke, but I laughed and laughed with her. She sat down on the bed. Her skin folded around her jolly face. She took my hand. ' You get out of here, hen. Another day in here and you'll think you *are* going crazy.'   She leaned closer, and whispered. ' Your story's all round the hospital, hen. I've heard the nurses talking. They're saying they cannae even find you on any of their CCTV footage, not a trace of you, leaving this ward, or going up to the roof. They haven't a clue how you got up there, hen. I think you're beginning to scare them. '

No a trace of me. And I knew why. I hadn't been here. I had become the ghost. I had been in Crete, letting Miss Baxter die.

Mum and dad came in shortly after. It was still early morning.   Dad 's face looked strained. Trying not to look worried.

' They want to keep you in another night,' mum said, ' because of the...sleepwalking....thing.'

I knew by the way she hesitated, they had also suggested it was something more than sleepwalking.

' Take me home, mum....' and to my relief it was my dad who answered.

' If she's going to...sleepwalk...I'd rather she do it in her own house. '

CHAPTER 29

Mum made me stay in bed, spoiling me the way mums do when you're not feeling well. Running back and forth with anything I needed.

Not that I wanted anything. I couldn't eat, couldn't read, couldn't watch television, couldn't concentrate on anything.

' You have to talk to us, Tyler,' mum said after one of her visits, sitting on the bed beside me. 'If there's something bothering you, you have to tell us about it.'

She waited for my answer. ' You don't really think someone pushed you under that truck.'

She didn't want the truth. How could she understand it, when I still didn't really understand it myself? She loved me, they both loved me, but she'd had enough of worrying about me. But I didn't want her thinking the alternative might be true either. ' You don't think I might have jumped in front of it, do you? You know I'd never do anything like that.'

A little hesitation, a second's pause. She was thinking of me being found on the edge of the hospital roof.

' Last night, I was sleepwalking, mum. I wouldn't have jumped. They gave me some kind of pill to help me sleep, and that made me sleep walk. '

I didn't tell her I had taken no pills. My head had been clear. That 'sleepwalk' could have killed me. If I'd taken one more step forward. It all rushed back at me. That moment when I had realised I was on the edge of that roof. I felt my colour drain from my face. Mum clutched at my hand.

' Are you all right?'

I assured her I was, told her I was just tired, wanted to have a nap. And after a few more moments fussing round me, she left. Once I was alone again, I had time to think. Why had Miss Baxter taken me back to the moment of her death? I had not stopped her dying. No matter what I did, she was still dead.

 Maybe, the message was that this time, there was nothing I could do. She knew that if I had, it would cause the...what did Mr. Clisham call it? The Butterfly Effect. If I had brought Miss Baxter back it would change too much.

I began to think it out. What if I *had* saved her life, brought her back, what exactly would have changed?

For a start, I would never have seen her that day in the supermarket, because Miss Baxter would not have died. She would still be alive, and I would never have got into all that trouble at my old school...so I would never have had to leave Grovepark. I'd still be friends with Annabelle....and....

I sat up in bed as my thoughts tripped faster through my head.

I would never have gone to St. Anthony's and that would mean Ben Kincaid would still be dead, and Father Michael, and I would never have met Jazz or Aisha or Callum and Adam or....I would never have met Mac.

NO!

Sorry, a million apologies Miss Baxter, but I couldn't save you, and I'm glad.

I didn't want to go back to all of that. I wanted my life the way it was now.

And maybe Miss Baxter knew it too. She hadn't expected me to save her. She wanted me to save the children. I still didn't know how. If I went to the police they would never believe me. Not me, not Tyler Lawless with the reputation I had. Saving those children was surely the Baxters' responsibility. It was up to them to expose these people, not me. Yet I knew there was still something she needed me to do.

She wasn't finished with me yet.

CHAPTER 30

My dad drove me to school next day. Wouldn't let me take another day off. I didn't want to. I wanted things to get back to normal. Dad was hardly talking to me, but he was worried. Worried that I was on the verge of suicide, worried I was on the verge of losing my sanity. Protecting me as he always had.

' I'm sorry I give you all this worry, dad.' I touched his hand on the steering wheel. His knuckles tightened white around it.

' Your good qualities make up for any of your bad.' He took his eyes off the road and smiled a strained smile at me.

' I'm going to be so good from now on. I promise.' I told him, and left him with a kiss on the cheek.

Dad dropped me at the gates of the school, at those ornate iron gates. There was something about this school I loved. Something linking me to it. It had brought out my gift. I didn't want to leave it. Leave the friends I had made here.

If I had saved Miss Baxter they would have been lost to me. The Butterfly effect would have lost them to me.

' Don't let anything happen today, Tyler,' Dad pleaded with me before he left.

I so wanted nothing to happen. Yet I had no control over events. Miss Baxter would be back.

No one asked about my ' accident.' But I could feel all eyes on me as I walked from one class to another. Tyler, up to her old tricks again, the text messages would be saying. Word had got round, as I knew it would that I had thrown myself in front of a truck, and I'd bet they knew all about the incident on the roof of the hospital. Tyler Lawless was getting even more weird. I tried hard to ignore them all.

Now, after what I'd said to Jazz, I felt even a chill with my friends. None of them asked about what happened at the hospital. They stayed by me, they supported me, but they were puzzled by my behaviour. I needed to make it up to Jazz. I felt so bad about the lie I had told her. I had hurt her feelings. I'd done it for the best of reasons. I wanted her safe, but I didn't want her to stop talking to me.

It was only at break I got a chance to speak to her. ' You can leave everything else about the party to me, Jazz.' I told her. ' You give me a list of everything else we have to get, and I'll get it. Promise.'

She didn't look too sure. She had hardly smiled at me.

' I'm sorry I told you lies, Jazz. It was a silly thing to do. It will never happen again. I promise. I know I've got a lot of making up to do.'

It was going to take more than an apology this time, but she nodded. ' Ok,' she said.

It was at least, a start.

First class after lunch was English. We were all hurrying to get there, the girls anyway. Not because we loved English, but because the new young English teacher, Mr. Curtis, was a doll. ' Well fit,' Jazz called him, and we all agreed. He was tall, with blond hair and he blushed every time the girls walked into his class, fluttering their eyelashes, gazing at him. Still too new to teaching to know how to handle us.

Jazz and Aisha were already at the door of the class. I thought they weren't even going to wait for me. But Jazz held back and looked round at me. ' Coming?' she nodded into the classroom. She knew some in the class would start whispering about me as soon as I stepped inside. There was still no smile, but she wouldn't let me go in alone.

' Loo,' I whispered as I stopped at the door to the girls' toilets. ' I have to go before class.'

It was all going to be okay. That was the way I felt. I could make it up to Jazz.

The bell rang and by the time I came out of the booth, the toilets had emptied. Everyone was hurrying off to their classes. I washed my hands, and pulled the door open, and I knew right away it had happened again. Because when I stepped out of the toilets I wasn't in the corridor of St. Anthony's and its alcoves with statues and its dark

panelled walls.

I was back in my old school. Grovepark.

CHAPTER 31

I stood for a moment, listening, trying to get my bearings. I was in the English corridor and as I listened I could hear the murmur of someone speaking. I followed the sound. I turned a corner, and there she was again, Miss Baxter, standing against the wall. She was on her mobile phone. How often had I seen her, just like this, making those mysterious calls. Now here I was and I could move close enough to hear what she was saying . She was upset and angry, not quite crying, but close to it.

' You would never have told me if I hadn't found out, would you ?' She pulled in a sob as she listened to whoever it was on the other end of the line. 'No. No. You're supposed to be my parents, and I don't know how you could do such a terrible thing. Well, I'm going to do something about it and nothing you can say is going to stop me. '

She closed over the phone, and without thinking I moved back out of her sight, as if she just might be able to see me. I backed round the corner, and turned.

Liz Cole was standing in front of me, blocking my way. She was looking at something on the notice board. Just then, she swung round. She was facing me. I didn't even blink, because she couldn't see me, could she?

' What are you looking at!' she snapped.

My mouth fell open. I couldn't say a word.

' I said, Tyler Lawless, what are you looking at!'

She *could* see me. But how? Wasn't I supposed to be invisible? What was happening?

' Who are you spying on now!' Her hair was coal black like her name. She might have been really pretty if her face hadn't worn a permanent scowl. She gritted her teeth and said again. ' Who are you spying on now!'

She grabbed my arm and pulled me toward her. She could see me! She could touch me! What was happening?

' You can see me?' How could she see me? No one ever did when I stepped back in time.

' What kind of weirdo are you? Of course I can see you.' She looked behind me, to where Miss Baxter had been standing. I glanced too. The doors to the next corridor were swinging closed, the shadow of a figure disappearing. Miss Baxter.

Liz Cole shook me. ' Spying on a teacher again. Ever heard of minding your own business? Did you think you could just listen in on other people's conversations, and nobody would notice? In your dreams.'

I pulled myself free of her. ' What's it to you!' I remembered how Liz Cole was always causing me problems when I was in this school, seemed to hate me for no reason.

Her eyes flamed with anger. She flicked at the badge on her blazer. It proclaimed she was a Prefect. 'I'm going to tell the head that you've been eavesdropping on a teacher....again!'

' You'd do anything to be head girl, wouldn't you.'

' Something you'll never be, Tyler Lawless.'

' Don't want to be!' I snapped back at her.

Liz tried to grab me again. ' Right! You're coming with me.'

How often had she tried to boss me around? She was good at manipulating people was Liz, but not me. She wasn't going to take me anywhere.

' I don't think so,' I said, standing my ground. And the next time she pushed me, I pushed back.

That only made her madder, and the next time, it wasn't so much a push, as a punch. It caught me on my cheek and I stumbled back. But I was angry too, and I ran at her. I wasn't letting Liz Cole off with anything. She was the one who had told the teacher that I had said Miss Baxter had committed suicide, got me into no end of trouble. She was the one responsible for the awful text messages that were being sent around the school. I said I would get her. And this was sweet revenge. I flew at her, grabbed at her hair and shoved her roughly against the wall.

' That's the only thing you're good at, isn't it, Liz. Grassing.'

She struggled against me. ' It's not grassing when I'm telling on scum like you.' And now she grabbed at my hair and yanked . We both stumbled. I tried to keep my footing but she crashed on top of me, and the next moment we were on the floor rolling around like two wrestlers in a ring. We punched and clawed at each other, our faces so full of anger.

A little group of pupils had gathered around us, cheering us on. Enjoying the spectacle.

And then I was being hauled to my feet. So was she. One of the older boys had me by the shoulders, another girl had Liz.

'You're in for it this time, Lawless, 'Liz said, wiping a trickle of blood from her lips. I looked around, pupils I knew were standing there, with a look on their faces I had seen so often. A look that said there was something weird and strange about me. Not one of them looked as if they were on my side.

' She's on her last warning anyway.' The boy beside me who had me by the arm let me go, as if he might catch something if he held on to me any longer.

I leaned against the wall, knocking the notice board askew . ' I don't understand how you can see me...how this is happening....' I was talking to myself but they could hear me.

' She's even weirder this time,' Liz Cole said. ' She thinks she's invisible.'

Comforting arms went round Liz. I was left alone. ' Come on, Liz, you have to report her.'

The boy tried to grab at me again. ' You too, you better come.'

I moved away. ' NO!'

But Liz and the others were already going off down the corridor. Liz was almost in tears by this time. Crocodile tears, nothing real about them. I watched them go. Never so mixed up as I was at that moment.

Why was I here?

Miss Baxter wanted me to hear that conversation she'd had on the phone. There was still something I could do. But how had Liz Cole been able to see me?

Automatically, I straightened the notice board. Something there caught my eye. I stared at it for a long time. In that moment I saw how I could change things right now, for better, or worse. It was all up to me.

I hesitated for a moment, and I made my decision.

CHAPTER 32

I made my way back to the girls' toilets and stood at the door for what seemed an age, scared to go back inside. What if I was trapped here? I prayed. ' Let me be back in my own time! Please let me be back.'

My eyes were closed as I pushed through the doors.

I peered though my lashes. The broken mirror, the green painted walls, the old fashioned cubicles.

I was back in St. Anthony's. I almost shouted with joy!

I stood inside for a moment, hardly daring to go back outside. What would I find there. When I finally stepped out into the corridor again, never had I been so glad to see those dark panelled walls, or the statue of St. Joseph in the corner.   I'd never felt so grateful to be back in my own time. Grateful to have escaped.

But afraid too. Because what had just happened, had never happened in the past. I'd never had a fight with Liz Cole, and I'd never stepped back in time and had people able to see me.

So exactly why had it happened then?

I looked sick when I went back into the classroom. I know I did. I felt shaky and hot. The gorgeous Mr. Curtis noticed right away and wanted me to go home.

' I'll be fine, sir,' I said, and he was satisfied at last to give me a glass of water and let me sit quietly.

Mac kept glancing across at me, mouthing the words. ' Sure you're ok?'

I smiled back, warmed by his concern. But some of the others didn't look quite so sympathetic. News of my leaping in front of a truck, ready to jump from a roof, had circulated round the school. The text messages saying I was weird and wicked didn't seem so strange now. I saw suspicion in their eyes. I had been gone too long from the classroom. So what had I been up to now?

As Jazz and Aisha and I walked down the path out of school, Jazz was going over a long list of things we still needed to get for Mac's party. She was almost back to her normal self.

' I told you, I would get them,' I said. ' I won't let you down this time.'

Jazz furrowed her brow. ' We're going to meet at five at the hall. Wee Father Brady is opening it up special for us. So we can start getting it decorated. You'll definitely be there?'

' I don't think you should even be back at school,' Aisha said. ' I think you should just go home and get to bed.'

' I was only kept in for observation,' I said, quickly. ' I wasn't really hurt. I'll get everything, ' I rhymed off all the things we needed. ' Balloons, banners, party poppers. I'll order the cake too. I'll get off the bus a couple of stops early. There's a bakery on the corner, and a pound shop nearby. I'll get my dad to run me to the hall for five. I'll be there. I'm fine, honestly.'

I wanted them to believe it. *I* wanted to believe it.

CHAPTER 33

But I wasn't fine. Of course I wasn't. All the way home on the bus all I tried to make sense of what had happened today. I had never had a fight with Liz Cole. Plenty of arguments, yes. But they had never descended into a fist fight. She wanted Annabelle as her best friend, and she was mine. She hated the stories I was always telling. The one about the French mademoiselle, who was her favourite teacher, seemed to bother her more than the rest. But actually fight with her?

No. Not that I could remember.

So why had I been taken back? To hear Miss Baxter's words? To learn about the 'something terrible' she was talking about? She had been talking to one of her parents. They were the ones who had done 'something terrible.' I couldn't get my mind off it, even after I got off the bus and headed for the bakery. I couldn't get those words out of my head.

Something terrible.

I turned the corner and almost fell over Anne. She was standing on the street, playing with a yoyo. She grinned when she saw me. ' Tyler!'

I didn't smile back. The last time I had seen her she'd been annoyed with me, and the next moment I was being pushed into the path of a truck.

' Did you know I was in hospital, Anne?' I asked her.

She looked genuinely shocked. 'No. What happened?'

' The other day at the bus stop. Someone pushed me and I fell in front of a truck. I can't believe you never saw it.'

She shook her head. ' Must have been after me and mum got on the bus.'

She stretched out her hand to me and I flinched. She looked hurt.

It was time, I decided, to find out the truth about Anne. ' Who are you, Anne?'

Her freckled face crumpled. ' Who am I? That's a daft question. I'm your friend...and you're mine, aren't you?'

I looked at her as if for the first time. I knew she had something to do with all this. I knew she had always had something to do with this. Her black hair was held back in a clasp, her woollen cardigan buttoned up wrong, her white socks and sandals. How old fashioned she looked. I had thought her mother wanted to keep her a child, no modern clothes or styles for her daughter, just like the mother herself. She was a lonely, sad little girl, with a dead sister, and she frightened me.

' Don't you want to be my friend anymore, Tyler?'

' I don't know anything about you, Anne. And you don't know anything about me."

She stamped her foot. ' You do. You know I've just moved here, and you know my mum and ...I even told you about my sister.'

' Anne, I don't want to hurt you, but how did your sister die?'

Her face went red. I had said the wrong thing. But I had to know. It took her a moment to answer me. 'She didn't actually die...' she gulped. ' I say she died because....it hurts too much to tell the truth. But because you're my friend....I'll tell you the truth.'

' And what is the truth?' I asked her.

Her eyes were filled with tears when she spoke again. ' She went missing, Tyler, my sister went missing, and they never found her.'

Another missing child. Was this why I kept seeing Anne.? Was I meant to bring back Anne's sister? Save them all? Was that what Miss Baxter was trying to get through to me? 'Save the children', she had said.

And suddenly it all seemed to become clear. I couldn't leave this with the Baxters. Because the Baxters already knew what was happing to those children. They were part of this kidnapping ring. That's why she wanted me to hear that conversation. So I would know. That was the something terrible they had done. Anne was still talking to me, but I couldn't even hear her. My mind was racing.

The Baxters had been part of it, taking children, kidnapping them. Perhaps Anne's sister had been one of those children. Miss Baxter had found out. She'd gone to Crete, because that's where the children were taken. And she had died there. And that was when the Baxters had tried to get out of this kidnapping ring. But by that time they were trapped too. They knew too much, and if they told what they knew, they would die.

Yet they couldn't be completely bad people. He had warned me I was in danger. He had tried to protect me.

' You're not even listening to me!' Anne's voice was angry. She had told me a secret, and I had seemed less than interested. I began to move away from her. 'What's wrong, Tyler? Where are you going!'

I didn't answer her. I began to run. She called after me, but I ignored her. No time to waste. I might be able to get your sister back, I wanted to say. Maybe that was why I kept seeing Anne. The Baxters had the answer, they knew everything, and I was going to make them tell me.

CHAPTER 34

Something was urging me on, telling me I had to hurry, time was running out. Miss Baxter was fading, growing weaker. The Baxters held the key, and I had to go there. Find out the truth at last.

Even as I ran, I felt someone was watching me, following me. I kept looking round, careful as I crossed streets, keeping close to the walls. I must have looked suspicious myself because I saw people looking at me, wondering what I was doing.

I was out of breath by the time I reached the Baxters' street. It was a typical autumn afternoon. A man chopping at his hedge in his garden, a woman pushing a pram, a few cars parked by the kerb. An old Ford, a blue Megane, shiny and new, a black Mercedes, a grey BMW with smoked glass windows. I knew my cars. I was a motor mechanic's daughter.

As I neared the house I could hear sounds from their back garden. The grass was being cut, the smell rose in the air, the scent of fresh cut grass. Last cut of the season. I pushed open the gate and made my way behind the house. Mr. Baxter didn't notice me at first, pushing his lawnmower back and forth, making straight even lines on his lawn. It wasn't until he turned to come back that he saw me. Anger flared in his face.

This time I didn't flinch. I said at once. 'What was the terrible thing you did?'

He came towards me at a run, flinging the mower aside so roughly it fell over. I was almost afraid. I imagined him lifting me and carrying me back out onto the street. Still I didn't move.

' Can't you leave us be!' he screamed the words at me.

' You did a terrible thing....and I think I know what it was.' His face lost all of its colour then. He stopped dead.

' It's time we told her, Edward.' A soft voice behind me. I swung round. The wild haired, slightly drunk woman who had flown down the hall at me stood in the doorway of their conservatory. She didn't look drunk, or wild haired now. She looked calm, serene. Her hair was pulled back too tightly from her face, it aged her. Her face was pale and without make up. ' You'd better come inside, Tyler.'

For a moment I didn't move. I wasn't afraid of them. They were too consumed with guilt about what they had done. They wouldn't hurt me. But I still didn't move, not till she said again. ' I think you should come inside...please.'

She stepped back, so I could move into the conservatory. It was hot in here. As I passed her she said. 'You've always been a part of this. I know that now.'

I couldn't understand what she meant. She ushered me to a seat. The sun streamed in, the room was lit with gold.

Mr. Baxter came behind us. I noticed that even at this time, he'd remembered to take off his muddy gardening shoes. He stood there in his socks, looking slightly comic. ' How does she know these things?' he said.

Mrs. Baxter didn't sit down. She stood looking down at me. ' She knows almost everything. Don't you, Tyler?'

I took a deep breath. ' I know something you did upset your daughter. Something terrible. I think I know what that something was. I know she went to Crete to find something out. And I know she was murdered there. I even know who murdered her.'

Mr. Baxter flopped into a chair. He said again. ' But how does she know these things>"

' All these missing children. You know what happened to them, don't you?'

As soon as I said that Mr. Baxter covered his face with his hands. He began to cry softly. His wife was still calm.

' You know a lot, Tyler. I think it's time you knew everything.'

CHAPTER 35

' My daughter was adopted, did you know that?' Mrs. Baxter said.

' No,' I said.

' We never told her.'

' And she was angry because you had never told her?'

Mrs. Baxter nodded her head.

' Why didn't you tell her?'

She seemed to be taking her time, giving herself courage to tell me the rest. ' There was a reason we didn't tell her she was adopted.' Mrs. Baxter's voice was flat. No emotion in it. ' A good reason.' She sat down at last, across from me, but still couldn't look me in the eye. Mr. Baxter sat slumped in his chair in the corner.

' I couldn't have children,' Mrs. Baxter went on. ' And we were always so desperate for a child. We tried to adopt, but they wouldn't let us. It isn't easy to adopt a child.' She stopped for a moment, as if it was hard for her to go on. ' I had a bit of a drinking problem then...' she glanced quickly at her husband, but he never even looked up. ' My husband's business took him all over the world, and I went with him....and then...his work took him to Crete. We found a private adoption agency there, that wasn't half as fussy as the ones in Britain. And we were offered this beautiful little girl...our daughter.'

Mr. Baxter spoke at last. ' We had to pay for her. A lot of money.'

' We didn't care,' Mrs. Baxter added quickly. ' I didn't care. I had my daughter.'

' It was an illegal adoption?' I said. 'You must have known that.'

' Yes, I suppose it was, but we didn't think of it like that at the time. We were told she had been born to a young girl who couldn't afford to keep her. The money was needed for this girl. She knew we could give her child a good home. ' Now she looked at me. Her eyes pleaded with me to understand. 'We honestly didn't think we were doing anything wrong. Not so very wrong.'

' And when Miss Baxter found out she went to Crete to find her birth mother?'

There was a long silence. Neither of them said a word, and I knew there was something more.

' If only it was that simple,' Mrs. Baxter said softly. She stood up. ' Wait a moment.' She went out of the room. I heard her footsteps go upstairs. Mr. Baxter and I said nothing to each other. His eyes fixed firmly on the floor. It seemed an age before she joined us again.

She had a piece of paper in her hand, yellowed, worn with age, it looked like a cutting from an old newspaper.

' This is the terrible thing we did, Tyler.' She held the cutting out to me. ' This is what she found out.'

The headline read :

LEAD IN MISSING CHILD STORY

Police have found a new lead in the Andrea Wilson case. The trail has led to Crete where there have been several reports of a girl answering Andrea's description. We can only keep our fingers crossed that at last this little girl is found and reunited with her distraught parents.

I read it twice before I looked back to Mrs. Baxter. ' Your daughter, Miss Baxter...she was this Andrea Wilson?'

Tears began to roll down her cheeks. ' We didn't know anything about it. Just a few weeks after we adopted her Edward's job took him to one of the other islands, and then the Middle East. We lived quietly, didn't read the British newspapers, didn't even have a television. I was totally wrapped up in my little girl. She changed our lives. ' She took a deep breath. ' I never drank again. She brought us so much happiness.'

' You didn't know anything about this little girl going missing?'

' By the time this newspaper report came out we had moved on. We honestly didn't know.' She turned to her husband. ' We tried to explain that to her, didn't we?'

' She didn't believe us. Couldn't blame her,' was all he said.

' Did she try to find her parents?' I asked.

' They're both dead. Her mother took an overdose of sleeping pills, couldn't come to terms with losing her baby. Her father remarried, but he died too, a few years ago.' She buried her face in her hands. 'It's a total tragedy, and it's all my fault.'

Her husband jumped from his chair came across to her and put his arms round her shoulder. 'Our fault. Our fault, dear.'

' But I don't understand why you didn't go to the police when you found this?'

' It was ten years before we came back to Britain. The story was long forgotten. I was doing an Open University degree and I was researching something and I came across this cutting in an old newspaper, and the more I found out, the more I knew our daughter was that missing child.' She looked right at me. ' But what could I do after all that time? The mother was dead by then, we were the only family my daughter knew.'

Mr. Baxter said. 'If we'd gone to the police we would have been arrested, and what would have happened to her then?'

' So you put the cutting away and tried to forget about it.'

Mrs. Baxter shook her head. ' No, not forget about it. Never forget about it.'

' So how did she find out?'

' She found the cutting, asked me about it, she knew I was trying to cover something up, lying to her, and when I finally told her what it was...she turned against us.'

' She was determined to find out who had taken her in the first place,' Mr. Baxter said.

' Nothing we could say would stop her...she was going to Crete to find out the truth...'

' And that's where she discovered it was still going on.' I said. ' Children were still being taken, and sold on .'

' And that was when the threats started.' Mr. Baxter said. ' To her, to us. Warning us to leave it be. But she didn't care. She said she was going to bring down this adoption ring.' Tears rolled down his face. 'But she didn't, did she? And she died hating us.'

And I hadn't been able to stop her dying, I thought.

'But I don't understand why you didn't go to the police when she died.' I said. ' You must have suspected she'd been murdered.'

Mr. Baxter answered. ' We planned to...but that adoption ring is still in operation. They let us know that if we went to the police, the child they had would be the one to suffer. And now they have another child, that little boy, and they warned us again when you started investigating. We're trying to protect another child. If we go to the police who knows what might happen. We don't know what to do.'

Mrs. Baxter let out a sob. ' If I had seen that cutting sooner, even after we left Crete, I would have taken her back. Back to her parents. I wouldn't let anyone go through that kind of heartbreak.' She reached out a hand to me. ' You have to believe me.'

I felt like crying too. I had got it all so wrong. Typical Tyler.

' There's something else you should know, Tyler, something I don't think you've worked out yet.'

What else could there be, I wondered?

She reached into the deep pocket of her cardigan and took something out. ' This is where I've kept that cutting, ever since I first found it.'

She opened her hand and I felt myself go faint when I saw what she held there. It was the lacquered box; Anne's lacquered box.

' You recognise it, don't you, Tyler? ' She opened the box and Carousel began to play. She took something from it. She handed it to me. It was a small green button. ' I believe this is yours,' she said.

CHAPTER 36

I stared at the green button. The button I'd given the little girl, Anne, just a few days ago. Then I looked back at Mrs. Baxter. Trying to take in the truth, not believing it.

' You're Anne.' I said at last.

She nodded. ' Yes, I'm Anne. That's why you scared me so much the first time I saw you. I couldn't believe it. I've had time to think about it, and I think I understand now.'

' But... I only saw you today...just before I came here...' yet, it was all becoming clearer. The old fashioned clothes, the hairstyle, the white socks, the patent shoes. Old fashioned, because she'd been from the past all along.

Mrs. Baxter sat beside me. ' When I was a little girl, I was always lonely.'

'You had a sister who disappeared,' I said.

' That's why I could never have let anyone go through what my mother and father went through. It broke their hearts. They were never the same.' She paused a moment before she went on.

'And when we first moved here, I felt so alone. I had left all my friends. There was no one....and then...you came along, Tyler. You talked to me, you were so nice. You helped me. I didn't feel lonely after you came into my life. But no one else ever saw you. They told me, I had an imaginary friend. That you didn't really exist. I had made you up to compensate for my sister. That's why I was always trying to get you to come and talk to them...to prove you really existed.'

' I know,' I said.

' And then, after a while, I found another friend and I stopped seeing you. I almost forgot all about you, believed you really had been an imaginary friend. Until that day you came here, and I recognised you...and I heard your name and....and I couldn't believe it was you. '

Yet, it was clear to me in a way she would never understand. Me, Tyler Lawless, who could move in and out of other people's time. I knew it was possible.

' Then I looked in the box, and I saw the button and I remembered, I remembered how I used to think, how could she be imaginary, and give me a button? ...and I knew then, and don't ask me how I knew, but I knew then that you had come to me for a reason. When I was a little girl you helped me, and you were back again, and I just knew you were here to help again. ' She reached across and gripped my hand. ' I don't know how. But I know you're going to make it all right.'

My head was filled with everything that had happened. It swirled round and round in my head. Miss Baxter going over that cliff, the hand pushing me into the path of that truck, meeting Anne, a yellowed clip from an old newspaper. And in the background the music for Carousel played over and over. Everything tumbled round in my mind. I began to feel dizzy.

' Are you feeling all right, Tyler?' Mrs. Baxter asked because of my silence.

I didn't answer her. Because it was as if everything, all the facts, everything that had happened over the last few days were putting themselves in order, helping me to see what I had to do. How I was meant to change things.

I could almost hear the click when they all finally fitted into place.

' Can I keep this?' I held the cutting out to Mrs. Baxter.

She folded my hand around it. ' Yes, of course'

I stood up. ' I know what I have to do now.'

She didn't ask me what. ' Be careful Tyler.'

I headed for the door. Mr. Baxter was there, he didn't tell me to be careful. He had listened to all his wife had told me, and he looked stunned. He would never believe it...and maybe, he would never have to.

I hurried down the path, and turned down the street. I felt as if I was in a countdown. I had to do what must be done, no time to waste. Miss Baxter was growing weaker.

Time. I was flitting in and out of it. Moving from one time to another. Not impossible at all. Not for me.

CHAPTER 37

The Baxter's tree lined street led onto a long lane, bright still with sunset gold filtering through the trees. A shortcut to where I was headed. All I had in my mind was what I had to do. When my phone rang in my pocket I was hardly thinking as I took it out. It was Jazz.

' Where are you? We've been waiting for you. We're at the chapel hall. Did you get everything?"

I knew by her tone she knew I hadn't. I hadn't even thought about it. I had forgotten all about meeting them. I hesitated and Jazz knew the answer. I heard her draw in her breath. ' I'm really trying here, Tyler, but you're making it really hard.'

'Look Jazz, I've got too much on my mind....' I wanted to tell her I'd make it up to her. She didn't let me finish.

She broke in, stopped me. ' You've got too much on your mind? It's always about you, Tyler. Some people have got real problems, Tyler. You're the one that's lying and pretending you see ghosts! Me and Aisha have done everything for this party.'

I was mixed up and scared, lame excuses for the way I snapped at her. ' Well, you were the smart alec who suggested the party, weren't you!'

' Oh right, is that what you think....' she was ready to rant at me, but I listened no further. I snapped the phone closed, just as I felt a hand on my arm.

' Sorry, don't mean to interrupt...but...'

I swung round. And found myself looking into beautiful dark blue eyes. Eyes I had seen before.

 The boy at the bus stop. He was smiling, and I automatically smiled back. ' You're the girl who fell, under that truck. Wow! Are you ok?'

I nodded. ' Yes, I'm ok.'

' Good,' he said. 'That could have been really nasty....'

I wasn't afraid. Even when I heard the purr of the car behind me. I didn't turn. The boy's hand moved me closer to the hedges to let the car pass on the narrow lane. At least, that was what I thought he was doing. What happened next happened so fast I didn't have time to think. The car came up beside me, a dark blue BMW, it flitted across my mind that I'd seen that car before. Didn't have time to register. The back door opened, a hand reached out. The boy with the dark blue eyes almost lifted me, and I was thrown inside.

I struggled. I lashed out. I kicked. But I was held fast. Strong hands gripped me, strong fingers nipped into my arms.

The man driving was older than the other two. He turned back for a moment. ' Be careful .Rick No bruising. No marks.'

The words didn't comfort me. They terrified me. What were they going to do to me?

Rick? I had heard that name before. It was who they had been talking to when I had travelled to Crete and saw Miss Baxter. Rick, the voice on the phone. Rick, the boy with the dark blue eyes.

I tried to twist round to see the other man who was holding me. I almost fainted. I had seen him before too. I was looking at the scarred face, the cold eyes, of the man who had killed Miss Baxter. Something else terrified me. Neither of them cared that I could see them, identify them. And that was because I wouldn't be here to identify them. That thought made me yell.

' Help!' I beat my fists against him, dug my elbows into his chest. I took them by surprise, one of my arms slipped free. I took my chance and drew my nails down Rick's face, and he winced and drew back. Bubbles of blood appeared on his cheeks. Good. I had marked him.

I had made him angry too. Those blue eyes of his flashed. ' Maybe one bruise won't matter,' he said. And he hit me so hard, I passed out.

CHAPTER 38

It was dark when I came to. Night had fallen. My mum and dad would wonder where I was-the first thought, and then almost immediately, my second thought. Where was I? It felt as if someone was thumping a rock tune inside my head. I was sure I was going to be sick. Dust and grit rubbed at my face. Somewhere close I could hear voices, the voices of men, harsh voices, couldn't make out at first what they were saying. My brain was a fuzzy ball of cotton wool.

I didn't move. Let them think I was still unconscious. Gave me time to think. Cold air blew against my face, and through broken windows I could see the sky, still with streaks of light there, not quite black with stars yet. I heard traffic on the street below. Distant traffic. Far below.

I knew then where I was. The old derelict sugar warehouse that stood by the docks. It had been fenced off. Too dangerous to go near after a storm had sent what was left of the glass in its windows crashing to the street below. Broken windows, gaping holes in the floors. Isolated. I looked down. Now I moved, couldn't help myself. Because I was on the edge of one of those gaping holes.

Something stirred in my memory. A dream, a nightmare. My nightmare....and I remembered how it ended.

I died.

' She's come to. Told you we shouldn't have waited.' I looked across. The three men were there, in the shadows.

' I wanted her to see.' It was this Rick who said it, and he moved closer. Out of the shadows, so I could see his face.

It bore the scratches I had made. He still smiled at me, but now there was a ruthlessness in that cold smile. I had been pushed in front of that truck, and he was the one who had pushed me. Heart like a stone. He came closer.

Stupid to even ask what they intended to do to me. Why waste words?

' It won't look like an accident, if that's what you're thinking.' My voice trembled though I tried so hard to keep it steady. 'I mean...what reason would I have for coming up here?'

' We've covered that,' he said.' There will be a good reason.' He held up my phone. ' You had a terrible argument with your friend, remember?'

He moved closer. I shuffled back and froze. Too, too close to that gaping hole.

' You've fallen out with her. I heard you. The last straw.' The light caught those dark blue eyes, how beautiful they were. He said. ' Everyone knows you were on the verge of taking your own life. Leaping in front of that lorry, ready to jump from that roof, and those text messages? They must have been so hurtful. ' He knew everything. ' After that quarrel , it was all too much for you...teenage suicides, they happen all the time.'

He held my phone over the edge of the hole. Let it drop from his fingers. ' There goes your phone. And, now, it's your turn.'

I wasn't going to make it easy for him. ' No one will really believe I could do this.'

He shook his head. ' Oh, come on, Tyler Lawless, they'll believe it. They know all about you. Weird and wicked, I think the texts said. Unstable too probably.'

' And I know all about you. In fact, I know too much, is that it? ' I was trying to keep him talking, trying desperately to think up a plan to save myself. ' You've been kidnapping children for years...'

He shook his head. ' Not me,' he said... ' it's what you might call, a family business. And we don't kidnap them. We...relocate them with other families. They all go to good homes. We're very fussy were they go. Families desperate for children. Families with money to pay. Lots of money. Everybody wins. That's not so bad is it?'

He said it as if he really believed he was offering some kind of humanitarian service .As If I would believe that.

' And Miss Baxter went out to Crete, and found out what you were doing, and you arranged a little accident for her. Pushing her car over that cliff.' I looked at the man in the shadows. ' You did that, scarface, didn't you? Drove her to the spot, pushed her and her car over.'

I heard his gasp . ' How did she know that?'

The older man's voice was harsh. ' Get it over with Rick, you're wasting time.'

Rick took a step closer. I struggled to my feet, too close to that edge. At last I had everything worked out, and now, it was useless. I was useless. And everyone would think my death was suicide, and if the Baxters tried to tell anyone otherwise, they would be dead too. And the child they had now...what would happen to him?

No!

I wasn't giving up without a fight. I had too much to lose. The floor around me was littered with debris. A broken plank wobbled under my feet. In a second I had swooped down and grabbed it. I did not waste another second, I held it like a baseball bat, and I ran at them.

I took Rick by surprise, I thudded into him and he stumbled, and when I walloped the scarred man on the knees his legs buckled and he went down. As he dropped I swung the bat again and hit him hard on the back of the head. The other one reached out to grab me, and I swung round and caught him hard on his outstretched hands. He yelped and drew back.

But Rick the youngest, the most dangerous of them, he had slipped behind me and before I had a chance to do anything he had his arms wrapped around me. I tried to swing at him, but I was held fast. He began to lift me back towards the edge. ' Time to go, little one,' he said.

I was going to die. I wasn't strong enough to stop him, no matter how I struggled. Already the other two were getting to their feet, their faces lined with anger. I could do nothing to stop them now. 'I'm sorry Miss Baxter!' I yelled it out. ' You should have asked somebody else to help you.'

' Who the hell is she talking to?' The scarred man looked round, but he was laughing at me. I was no danger to him now.

I tried desperately to struggle free, but Rick, with the deep blue eyes, he was too strong for me. He held me in a clamp like grip.

Inches from the edge. Seconds from death.

Nothing could save me now.

CHAPTER 39

A sudden wind sent paper and rubble blowing across the floor. There was a fire escape behind the other two, and the door there blew open, then slammed shut again with such force it startled the two men and they twisted round.

' What was that!'

' Do it!' the older man turned back quickly and yelled to Rick. Then he swung round. He clutched at his arm. ' Something grabbed me there!'

The scarred man felt it too. He touched his face. ' Who's there! Who did that?'

Both of them swivelled round, this way, that way.

The scarred man jumped. ' It's touching me.' He looked all around. ' Something's pushing me.'

He began to stumble towards us, his feet sliding on the floor. He struggled to stop himself. 'Something's pushing me.'

Rick looked back at them but he still didn't loosen his grip on me.

' Get it to stop!' The scarred man was yelling now, his hands trying to catch hold of something to stop himself.

And then, I saw what they couldn't see.

Miss Baxter.

There she was, moving silently, blowing her icy breath towards him. Forcing the scarred man backwards with her ghostly hands.

Rick swung me round to face him. ' What are you doing!' he shook me by the shoulders. ' What are you doing!'

They thought it was me who was doing this. Well, let them.

The scarred man stumbled and fell on his back. He looked terrified. ' Tell her to stop!'

' Let me go then,' I said. My voice sounded sure and unafraid.

Rick shook me so roughly that the whole floor seemed to shake as if a tremor had run through it. 'Stop what you're doing now!' and for the first time, his cockiness had vanished. I saw real fear in his eyes.

Miss Baxter loomed over the man on the floor, the man who had killed her, and now she looked like the ghost she was, an avenging angel, roaring with anger. He couldn't see her, but some ancient understanding told him she was there. Told him that something was there. He scrambled back, and even I, watching him, let out a scream. He was too near the edge. He turned and realised it too. Debris and dust fell before him.

He looked down. Tried desperately to get a grip of what was left of the floor. Nothing for him to grip, nothing to cling on to. And in that final second before he fell, I was sure he saw her too. Saw her hovering over him. Saw the ghost of the woman he had dragged to her car, and pushed down into the sea. Such terror could not have been caused only by his fear of death. He saw her, just as he toppled head first into the black chasm where I was meant to go.

He fell, just as Miss Baxter had fallen, tumbling over and over.

His dying scream filled the night air, fading into darkness. Rick's fingers bit into my arms. ' Who are you?'

He thought I had caused this. They all thought I had caused this. Now he was afraid of me. The older man yelled and there was terror in his voice. ' Throw her over, let's get out of here. Someone must have heard that scream. The police will be here...aaggh!'

Even as he spoke, he was lifted from the ground. He had no control over his movements. There was terror on his face. Only I could see who was lifting him. Miss Baxter.

Then she dropped him to the floor. That was the moment Rick slackened his grip on me. I took the chance, shook myself free of him. I kicked out, caught him on the shin and he stumbled back. I ran. I saw her ghostly face urge me on. I heard no voice, yet the words she spoke were as clear to me as if she had shouted them out. " Run! Do what you have to do.'

Rick was right behind me. The other man still lay on the floor where Miss Baxter had dropped him, too terrified to move. Rick was inches behind me. I could feel him close to me. I could feel his anger too. It seemed the fire escape was too far. I would never make it.

As I pulled open the door, he was almost on me, his fingers brushed against my back.

Then, there was a gasp and I glanced back, only a glance, only for a second, and she had her ghostly hands encircling his neck. He tried to claw at them, but touched nothing, and the terror of those unseen hands made him cry out and fall to the ground. Miss Baxter looked at me. She knew what I needed to do. I read that in her eyes. I ran out of the fire door, and as soon as I stepped outside, the door slammed shut.

CHAPTER 40

Miss Baxter had come back to help me. She had given me the chance to change things, the way they were meant to be changed. My feet clattered down the fire escape stairs, my whole body shook. I heard a scream. A man's scream. What was going on in that room above me? Whatever she was doing, she was doing it to protect me, giving me time to do what I had to do.

At last I was out of the building. I hurried across the waste ground, to the street. The town seemed deserted. No one was around. Shops were all closed, except for the little Tandoori takeaway. No sound of the approaching police. The man who had fallen, had landed inside the building. If no one had heard his scream, he could lie there for days. The way, perhaps I had been meant to lie. Unfound. Alone.

I had never run so fast, hardly checking for traffic as I crossed the road at the church and headed up towards the west end of the town. I stopped for a second, sure I could hear running footsteps behind me. But they were only the echo of my own. The town grew even quieter here, the moon was hidden behind the heavy clouds. It was dark. Night time, yet I knew she would be waiting for me. Anne. Mrs. Baxter when she was a girl. Drifting into my time, as I had drifted into hers.

My heart pounded. I wanted to stop, but I was afraid to. I knew there was no time to waste.

At last I was on Anne's street, and there she was, as I had known she would be. Standing at her window, watching for me.

She looked up when she saw me coming. Her face broke into a smile. She waved, and I beckoned her down. She was out of her tenement close in a moment. She ran to me.

' I knew you would come.' She grabbed at my hand. She looked as if she'd been crying. ' I've been watching for you for ages. I'm so sorry I got angry at you. I shouldn't have said those things. You've been so nice to me. You have to come in and see my mum, Tyler . She doesn't think you're real. Nobody thinks you're real.' She tugged at my hand.

' I can't come in today, Anne.' I leaned against the wall, trying to get my breath back.

She screwed up her little face, peered closer. ' Have you been running?'

' Yes, I've been running. Running to see you. There's something I want you to do, Anne.'

Her face brightened even more. ' I'll do anything for you, Tyler.'

I took the cutting from my pocket. ' I want you to put this in your treasure box, you know, that special box you showed me. I want you to put it right on the bottom, as if it was the lining of the box.'

She took the piece of yellowed paper from me. ' What is it? It looks old.' She was disappointed. ' I'm not a very good reader...what does it say?'

' It doesn't matter what it says. Not now. But one day it will. And when you read it, you'll understand.'

I could see she couldn't understand now. Her brows creased in a puzzled frown.

' Will you do this for me, Anne? It's the most important treasure you will ever have.'

' Of course I will.' She had a bag slung round her shoulder, and she opened the clasp and drew out the box. ' I took it with me to show you I still had your button. That I hadn't thrown it away because we fell out.' She opened the box and held out the button for me to see. ' Do you want it back?'

I shook my head. ' No. Keep it, Anne. It's yours. '

She beamed a smile at me, and with her small hands she folded the cutting and placed it very carefully at the bottom of the box. Then she put her other treasures on top of it. The earring, the coin, the silver bangle, and my button. She looked back at me. ' Just like that?' she said.

I touched her hand. ' That's perfect.'

' Anne! Anne!' It was her mother's voice.

' Oh I must tell you, I've made a new friend. Her name's Laura. She lives next door.'

 Any moment now Anne's mother would appear at the window, she would see I wasn't there. There was no one there with Anne. Anne believed in me, I had to keep it that way. ' Didn't I say you would? I'm so glad, Anne.'

She slid from the wall. ' Will I see you again, Tyler?'

' You don't need me now,' I said. ' Now you've got a friend.' A real friend, this time, not an imaginary one. A friend her own age.

' I'll never forget you, Tyler.'

' I know you won't.'

' Anne!' her mother appeared at the mouth of the close, that harsh voiced woman who never seemed to smile. No wonder, when she had already lost one child. ' What on earth are you doing out there at this time of night! Come in here right now!'

That's when I remembered how late it must be. ' Go ,you should be home.' I told her again. I touched her hand.

Anne looked back at me once. She smiled and waved, and I stepped behind the bushes out of her sight. I'd never see her again, not like this. But I knew Anne would carry on with her life, and I would become a vague memory. She would begin to believe I *was* that imaginary friend, until that time when she would adopt a baby in Crete, and she would remember that cutting I had given her, and she would open the box and take it out, and she would read it, and she would know what she had to do.

' If I'd seen this cutting sooner I would have taken her back to her real parents.' Hadn't Mrs. Baxter told me that? ' I would never have let them suffer the way my mother and father suffered.'

And when the grown up Anne would read that article, she would know who the baby she had adopted really was. Andrea Wilson, the little girl who had gone missing. She would take her back to her real family, tell the police how she had got that baby, and the adoption ring would be caught, and none of those other children would have been abducted. They would all be saved. Miss Baxter wouldn't have died her unlawful death and so I would never have seen her in the supermarket and I wouldn't have had to leave school, and wouldn't have gone to St. Anthony's ....and Ben Kincaid would still be dead.

I clutched at my head. It went on and on, just as the teacher had told us, the butterfly effect. I had changed everything.

It had to be done to save those children, I knew that. But I had promised myself I would search out my friends at St. Anthony's I would still find them. Somehow, I would make things all right.

I stood at the corner of the street, almost in tears, waiting for that moment, the moment that always came when time changed. Waiting for the world to swirl and turn around me.

Instead, out of nowhere, Rick leapt in front of me. Before I could move he had grabbed my hair, dragged me towards him. He looked like a wild man, his hair unkempt, his leather jacket torn. He was covered in dust. His dark blue eyes were shining with anger, and fear. I saw the knife in his hand. It gleamed in the light from the street lamp.

' Forget the accident, they can find you tomorrow, with your throat cut. '

And I felt the cold steel of his blade at my throat.

CHAPTER 41

Light exploded through the clouds, bright as day. And I knew it had begun. But was it too late for me?

Rick stumbled against me, and the razor sharp blade nicked my skin. I gasped with fear. The air was all at once filled with a deathly silence. It grew dark as suddenly as it had been light. He stepped back, pushed me from him. The world began to spin. Rick staggered, couldn't keep his balance. He stared at me, his eyes filled with what I can only call, terror. The knife shook in his hand. He saw no fear in me, and that scared him even more.

' What have you done?' He looked all around him, for now the street had disappeared. We were engulfed in a weird kind of fog, and it was swirling all around us. ' What's happening?' He screamed it at me. Then his voice changed and there was real fear in it. His cry was a scream of terror. ' Who are you!'

He never got his answer-though I would never have told him. At that second the fog seemed to close in on him, swallow him up, and he was gone.

The dust settled. It was still night. I heard a fog horn on the river. The world was back to normal.

I should have been elated. I had done it again, after all. But I wasn't. I felt only sadness. In this world, I had no Jazz, no Aisha....and no Mac.

I began to run. I had to find out what I had changed.

Mum was at the window watching for me as I ran up the street to our house. Worry and anger shared a space on her face. Joined, when she saw me, by relief. By the time I reached our gate she had thrown the front door wide open. ' Tyler, Where have you been! I've been worried sick about you. Your dad and Steven are out looking for you.'

I had no answer, because what could I say? ' I lost my phone...' all I managed to mumble.

Then I burst into tears. Too much had happened I could never explain. Too much for a young girl like me to cope with. Less than an hour ago a man had held a knife to my throat. I could still feel the ice cold blade. I felt my skin for the nick he had made. But there was nothing. Of course there was nothing. It had never happened.

But it had.

Mum pulled me into the living room. ' Let me call your dad. He's worried sick about you too.'

I still cried as I listened to her explaining that I was home, and no, she didn't know why I was so late, and we could find out in the morning, but I was fine.

She sat on the sofa beside me when she came off the phone. ' Where have you been, Tyler?'

I was trying so hard to think what I could tell her.

' I think I know what happened,' she said, taking me by surprise. ' You fell out with your friend, didn't you?'

Still I said nothing. She smiled, squeezed my hand. ' She feels bad about it too. She's blaming herself for you not coming home. You better give her a ring. Let her know you're safe.' Mum handed me the phone. 'Here, call her.'

I must have looked incredibly stupid. Mum shook her head. ' Always in another world, Tyler. Call her, she wants you and her to make up.'

At last I found my voice. 'Annabelle?'

Mum rolled her eyes. ' Annabelle? When was the last time she was your best friend? Call Jazz , of course. Who else?'

CHAPTER 42

Jazz ? But surely Jazz wasn't my friend any longer. I had changed all that. My fingers trembled as I punched in her number. She answered it at once, obviously waiting for my call. I could almost picture her in her bedroom, sitting cross legged on the bed. She sounded so relieved to hear my voice. 'Oh Tyler, I've been worried sick.' She didn't give me a chance to answer her. ' It was all my fault. I shouldn't have lost my temper. That's me all over. I flare up, didn't mean to.'

' I didn't get the stuff for Mac's party...?' had that argument had still happened?

I heard her sigh. ' I know, but that's all right. I got them. I knew you'd forget. You're always in a dream, Tyler.'

' Am I?'

There was a giggle of relief in her voice. ' Course you are. But that's just you. And we can go and check out the hall tomorrow night. Where did you go, Tyler?'

What could I tell her? ' I just walked, that was all....'

' Typical Tyler, and here, I had you jumping in front of a lorry or getting your throat slit...and you're supposed to be the one with the imagination. '

If only I could tell her how right that imagination of hers had been.

' Jazz? Do you remember that teacher I told you about from my old school?'

' The one that got you expelled?'

' Yes, that's her, Miss Baxter...'

' Miss Baxter? Was that her name....?'

' Yes.'

' Oh. I thought she was some French bird?'

'French?' I jumped to my feet. What was she talking about?

' Have I got it wrong? Was it not because that Liz Cole bird kept grassing you up about that French mamselle that you got into all that trouble?'

There had been no Miss Baxter. Not now. No dead teacher. I'd had to leave my old school because of my stories about the French mamselle...and Liz Cole telling on me, of course.

' It was the French teacher...' I said, understanding at last.

There was a long dramatic sigh. ' You're not supposed to get Alzheimer's till you're old, Tyler.'

I began to smile. ' I know, but I'm fine. Better than fine. I'll make it up to you, Jazz. I promise. I will never be in a dream again.'

' Yes you will,' she answered me. ' and see if you're not, I'll know you're not the real Tyler!'

CHAPTER 43

How had it happened? I didn't know, and I didn't care. It didn't matter. I'd still left my old school, under a cloud, because of my stories about the French mamselle. I still had gone on to St. Anthony's. I had still saved Ben Kincaid. And Miss Baxter hadn't died.

In my room, I opened up my laptop and trawled through the internet looking for stories connected to Andrea Wilson.

And there they were. Tons of them. The little girl snatched in a London park. For weeks it was the front page story, as they followed lead after lead. And the trail lead to Crete. Then the biggest headline of all. The baby had been found. The couple, a Mr. And Mrs. Baxter, had adopted a baby in Crete and when the woman had read an article about that kidnapped child she had immediately notified the police, handed the child back, and brought down an international adoption racket. The whole story was there, with photos of the Baxters and the Wilsons.

' I had to hand her back,' Mrs. Baxter was reported as saying. ' I had a sister who went missing. So I know the pain it causes. If someone had snatched my baby, I couldn't bear it.'

The families had remained friends, a follow up story said. Mrs. Baxter had remained a part of Andrea Wilson's life.

It was what I had wanted. What I had prayed for.

I thought about what Mr. Clisham had told us about the Butterfly Effect. And it was right. But there was something else I had figured out. Miss Baxter was meant to live. And I was meant to go to St. Anthony's and save Ben Kincaid.

I hadn't so much changed the past, as put it back the way it was meant to be.

And I realised something else too. Right at the moment when I was sure I had done as much as I was able, Miss Baxter had come to me, led me back into my old school, Grovepark. It hadn't been the figure of Miss Baxter I had seen disappearing through the doors. It had been the French teacher. And Liz Cole and I had fought, and she had marched straight to the head's office and that fight had been the last straw. After that, they were happy to see me leave.

That day, Miss Baxter had helped me to put things back the way they were meant to be.

CHAPTER 44

Mac tried to look surprised the night of his party. Adam brought him into the hall, blindfolded, and we all leapt up and yelled. ' Happy Birthday!' and the blindfold was whipped off and his eyes, those lovely deep brown eyes of his, went wide, as if he hadn't had a clue about it.

' You should be an actor,' I told him.

' Maybe I will be. Who knows?' he said.

' This party has cost us a fortune. I hope you appreciate it.' Jazz said. ' The banners, the balloons, the little things on sticks, the cocktails....'

' Diluting orange with an umbrella stuck in it.' Adam said, holding up one of the 'cocktails' in its plastic cup. ' Hot dogs, sausage rolls. You really know how to throw a party, Tyler.'

' I can't take any credit,' I said. ' It was all Jazz and Aisha. I was rubbish.'

' You were just Tyler, dreamy Tyler.'

Jazz laughed and looked over at Callum and Aisha, love's young dream They were in a corner of the hall. Gazing into each other's eyes, moving to the music.

' Call that dancing!' Jazz shouted.

They both turned, startled and Callum's face went brick red.

' And call that music!' Adam yelled. ' Get some decent cds on, Mr DJ!'

True to his word, wee Father Brady joined us. Our unofficial chaperone. He walked around the hall, hands behind his back, moving in time to the music, asking if everyone was having a good time.

' Can you not get rid of him?' Adam asked Jazz.

' Think yourself lucky he's not asked you to be an altar boy,' she said. I thought he only added to the fun.

Jazz nudged me. 'Hey! Look what the cat's just dragged in.'

It was Annabelle, and with her, Liz Cole. I had asked for them to be invited, but hadn't thought they would come.

' That Liz Cole's got a face you would love to stuff in a pie,' Jazz whispered.

 Annabelle came right up to me. ' Thanks for asking us, Tyler.'

But I had my reasons. ' How's that Miss Wilson at your school?'

Miss Wilson, who had once been Miss Baxter. I had learned she was a teacher there, Just as she was meant to be.

' Oh, she's lovely.' Her voice became a whisper. ' You should write a story about her Tyler. Did you know she was kidnapped when she was a little girl?' And she babbled on about the story I knew already.

She smiled at Mac and handed him a gift. ' Happy Birthday.' And she drew Liz into the conversation. Did she never smile I wondered? ' Liz is celebrating as well. She's just won a place in the area finals.'

' Oh, you went in for the X factor?' Jazz sneered.

Liz Cole sneered back. ' Actually, I'm a gymnast.'

' Oh, you roll about on a mat then?'

' It's a bit more than that actually. You've got to be an athlete to understand.'

Did that sneer ever leave Liz's face? She looked smug. She was better than we were. She was going to be a champion one of these days. That was what that look said. And she would never know that she owed it all to me.

Do you know what I did for her? Can you remember? That day I had gone back in time to my old school, the day we had had that fight? I had seen Liz Cole at the notice board. And when I looked there I saw that she had been putting her name up for the school trip. The trip to Aviemore where she would break her leg and ruin her chances of competing in championship competitions again. I thought about what I should do that day for a long time. I could have left her name there. But I couldn't do that. I had the chance to change her life too, for the better. I had taken her name off the list. So Liz hadn't been included in the school trip. She hadn't had the fall that had ruined her dreams.

I didn't like her. I would never like her. But I had had the chance to help her, and I did.

I was finding out more about this gift I had. Here was another thing that I had learned I could do.

I saw Liz take a long look at Mac, the sneer left her face, she tried a smile. I moved closer to Mac. Don't even think about it, Liz, I thought.

She raised an eyebrow and moved off with Annabelle. ' She's a bit of all right," Adam said. And Jazz choked on her drink.

' Jealous, Jazz?' I whispered.

She refused to admit it. ' I'd have to be committed first,' she said, and we all laughed.

I felt so good that night. My friends all there, Mac's arm round my shoulders. Miss Baxter alive and well, all thanks to me. Life was great.

Let the unlawful dead come, I said to myself. I'm ready. I'm here. If I can help you, I will.

I didn't have to wait long.

EPILOGUE

The night was almost over, people were drifting off home. Only stragglers were left in the hall as we began to clear up, filling up black bin bags with paper cups and plates and left over food. I was taking a black bin bag through to the kitchen when I saw her. A girl, standing by the door, pale as death itself. Her dirty blonde hair hung in long greasy strands. She stretched out her arms to me. And I saw that she was scarred on both her wrists. Long, ugly, jagged scars.

'Help me, Tyler.'

Her voice seemed to rasp in her throat.

I reached towards her. ' I will.' I said.

THE END

TYLER LAWLESS WITH BE BACK IN

SCARRED TO DEATH